Morris Malarky

Marshall Coombs

ISBN 978-0-9556475-6-7

All characters appearing in this work are fictitious. Any resemblance to real persons living or dead is purely coincidental.

Published by Marshall Coombs in association with Hedingham Fair

Printed in Great Britain by
The Five Castles Press
Ipswich

www.hedinghamfair.co.uk

To Glenda Beer
Maid of Barum

Summer

MORRIS MALARKY

Summer

Chapter 1:
Meet and Retire

'Now burn the photo.'

Zoe saw Ray's frown. He hesitated. She nodded encouragement.

'Hold on to your wish. I mean really visualise Alex mucking things up, and chant the spell to yourself. Then burn the image. Watch him diminish.' Her dark eyes were intent, large in her pale face.

'Does it matter that I can't really believe this works? It's not what I expected, somehow.' Ray had wanted... what? A bit of atmospheric magic? The bus shelter on Larksea promenade wasn't quite a moonlit grove, pleasant though the July night was. The seagulls were silent, the surf scarcely whispering. He pulled uneasily at his goatee beard. Zoe saw the shift in his sharp blue eyes, slightly hooded beneath his straight eyebrows. She tapped his knee lightly.

'Look, you don't want people admiring Alex's slack way of teaching morris any more than I do. That's the key. We're not harming him, just trying to influence events around him. The spell simply acts out your thoughts, and it's the change in you that matters. The effect ripples out from that.'

There *was* something witchy about her, thought Ray, admiring her long black hair tied back with a turquoise scarf. He knew of Zoe's interest in magic, or wicca as she called it, but hadn't thought a conversation at morris practice that week, where he had sounded off about Alex Tavener being both bossy and imprecise, would take this turn. He was intrigued enough to cut off part of a picture of Alex dancing from an old morris photo, and brought it to the pub later in the week at Zoe's insistence. Now they must get back to the others in the bar before their absence became noticeable.

'OK, up in smoke you go, you complacent bastard.' Alex withered before Ray's eyes. The acrid smell made his nostrils flare.

Zoe lifted her chin and twisted her fingers in her hair. 'So, Mr Ray Jenner, welcome to the circle of wicca.' Her taut smile sent a tingle down Ray's spine.

He thought: maybe I have started something.

*

Lolly Hayward was having the sort of morning when you feel scratchy. Nothing was wrong, exactly, but she had burnt the toast, ironed a fine crease into her favourite blouse, and couldn't find the coco pops.

'But I don't like cornflakes, you know I don't, dad!' wailed Naomi, trying to attract Ray's attention away from breakfast tv. She was nine years old, not Lolly's daughter, and not at her sweetest before school, either. For someone like Lolly, with her neat clean jeans, short brown hair carefully cut, and a peaceable nature which could usually bring order out of the domestic mess of their rented maisonette, Naomi's mood shouldn't have been a challenge.

'Never mind, darling. It's Friday. Swimming club tomorrow. Think of that.'

'I've got to get through Friday first,' sulked Naomi. 'We've got a maths test.' She scraped her chair and ran upstairs.

'Bother,' said Lolly, trying to engage Ray. 'I didn't mean to say that. I wanted to persuade her to come to the dancing on Saturday. That pub's got a good playground. I'm sure she'll enjoy that, little ball of energy that she is. I particularly want to dance Step'n'Fetch Her, now everyone's got the feel of it, and I'm down to play melodion at the craft fair in the castle in the afternoon, so I can't dance then.'

'Perhaps she could spend the day at Tamsin's. She goes swimming, doesn't she?' Ray smoothed the point of his beard, not wanting to be bothered with Naomi while he was out with the morris. As the manager of an estate agent's, he was more concerned about his morning visit to a seafront property. He had some ideas about how to get the vendors to drop their price.

Lolly bridled. 'Why don't *you* take her swimming for a change? You could bring them both on to the stand in the castle afterwards.'

'And miss the pub at lunchtime? My working man's reward! I know. Why not get Naomi to bring Tamsin along. They're thick as thieves and you can sell it to them as a treat.' Lolly sighed, wrong-footed by a helpful suggestion, unusual for Ray. She knew it would be up to her to make the arrangements, as well as drive, but they owed Tamsin's parents a day off, and the girls would certainly enjoy it.

'OK, I'll talk to her on the way to school.' She called upstairs. 'Are you getting ready, Naomi? I've got a surprise for you!' Now she must get Naomi's lunch box ready, and then get herself off to *The Body Shop*. She enjoyed her work, moving deftly amongst the elegant displays of fragrant products, but the new tills were a nightmare. And would Ray go to the pub again after work? The day was out of tune.

*

Brandon Corfield, tall and broad-shouldered with a shock of brown hair, had a confident physical presence and a quick eye that meant he could dominate his classroom at Mayfield School without apparent effort.

It was a hot afternoon, near the end of term, and the class were looking for distraction. What was young Sylvie doing at the back? He saw her get up and move to the window, undoing the top button of her blouse. She winked at Matt in the front row, and he began to chant *The Stripper*. A couple of the boys picked up the tune and several others started to join in. Heads turned towards Sylvie to see what was going on. Enjoying the response, she moved to the next button down.

Brandon smiled. He knew this lot well enough to joke with them and take a few risks. 'Sylvie! Don't be a drama queen and hog all the limelight. It's Matt's turn. Come on Matt, out here now, get your shirt off.'

Some of the girls jeered. Matt's embarrassment was a picture, and Sylvie grinned and applauded.

'OK everyone, enough of this now. Put your books away. I'm going to show that video I mentioned, about the Liverpool Poets. Questions afterwards. Matt, could you come and work the video for me?' Matt was pleased and bustled about the task while the class settled to watch.

Brandon let his mind wander, as eager for the bell as his pupils. Friday. The weekend. Dancing. Beer. He decided to finish promptly so he could pick Zoe up from the headmaster's office where she worked and get home in good time. Being at the same school was sometimes an advantage.

*

Zoe had her serious and concerned face on, but was seething inside. The headmaster was in his lecturing mode.

'So you see, Mrs Corfield, I can't just ignore a written parental complaint about you. Had Mr Clark telephoned, I would have done what I could to pour oil on troubled waters. But they're a solid, respectable family and –'

'But "bossy and overbearing" headmaster!' Zoe's chin was up, and she knew the effect a toss of her long black hair could create. She smoothed it now as she smiled. 'You know I'm not really like that. I can be direct, and I have to be sometimes, but parents can lose all sense of humour over their little darlings. You've encountered the Clark girl before. She can be very pert.'

'Ah yes. She called your husband a... yes, well, I remember now. Well, find a few words of explanation about the situation and spell out the girl's actual words, and I'll add something polite and conciliatory.' The head, who knew his secretary well, was quite capable of hiding behind her, if necessary.

A nod from Zoe, and he went back into his inner sanctum. Bloody little brat, she said to herself. It's the end of a long week and I could do without this. Chill, Zoe, chill. I need to relax tonight. Brandon can cook, or get a takeaway if he feels he can afford it. I've got to wash those new white trousers tonight and get ready for Saturday. At least that looks promising. Nice pub and there's that batik stall at the craft fair in the afternoon. And Ray will be there. I'll tell him what Carol was saying about Alex. Mustn't exaggerate too much or he'll think I'm manipulating things to make it seem as if our little ritual has worked already. But she did say Alex was all legs and no arse. I'll get Ray to sound out a few of his cronies. Plenty of time at the pub.

She fumed on. Bossy and overbearing. How dare they. Straightforward and perceptive more like. And subtle and influential. Watch out Alex.

*

Alex and Hannah Tavener were deep in conversation in their spacious kitchen.

'I don't think the men dance down to the women. In some ways the women are more precise and it's brought the men's dancing together.' After eighteen months as foreman, Alex was feeling a bit defensive about the side's style. He kept adjusting his glasses and rethreading them through his sideburns.

'I'm not saying it doesn't work the other way round, too,' Hannah replied. 'I've certainly tried to match Brandon's height in the capers, and most of the women have put more oomph into it this summer. It's just that I feel there's still something lacking, a sort of performance kick, you know, a flourish that makes the public and the dancers go – ' she threw both arms out – 'Yeah!' She smiled her big blonde smile.

They both enjoyed this kind of debate, especially on a Friday night with the children in bed and the better for a bottle of wine. The cares of the week receded rapidly, Hannah free from her part-time work at a solicitor's, Alex from his council job. Any aspect of the morris interested them. There was plenty to chew over. The side had voted to go mixed a couple of years ago, and there had been some heated exchanges about the advantages and disadvantages. A notorious letter in *The Daily Telegraph* titled *'It's a man thing'* had once asserted that the morris was a ceremonial dance for men only, men sworn to manhood, fiery ecstasy, ale, magic and fertility. The phrase 'It's a man thing' had become a running joke between the two of them, but that didn't mean they couldn't take some of the points seriously. Alex had a preference for the ecstasy and ale side; Hannah was intrigued by the suggestions of magic and fertility.

'I'm going to tell everyone to put a big surge into the cross caper in Step'n'Fetch Her tomorrow. If you want flourish, that's a natural, exuberant moment.' Alex was relishing the picture. 'It's a real showpiece when the two greeting each other match their movements and get a good height. I can't hope for the hanging-in-the-air effect, but everyone's enjoying that dance at the moment. If we're both in it, we'll have to blaze a trail.'

'Hope my ankle's up to it. Zoe will insist on being in it. You may have to surge with another partner!'

'Don't talk about surging. There's a lot of gossip going on at the moment. All sorts of little muttered conversations. Practice night's getting like the plot of *The Archers*. Some of it's personal and some of it's just pre-AGM politics. Oh well, if it means a bit of competition between people that brings up the level of the dancing, it's not such a bad thing, I suppose.'

'Ah ha, have you heard anything new?' Hannah was surprised. Alex wasn't given to gossip.

'Not really. Zoe was overheard sounding off about some of the men, including me. She gets into a corner with Ray and they make mischief.'

'Nothing new there then. She's a really good dancer but can't stomach others getting compliments. As long as she's not mounting an attack of some sort, like she did on Amy Kershaw last year. Amy really tries but rhythm's not her strong point as you know. She's an easy target. I'm still glad Pete had such a go at Zoe.' Pete Kershaw was one of the side's musicians, and the fallout from his row with Zoe was still echoing on.

'Everyone knows Zoe's a stirrer. It's not dangerous. Come on, Mrs Tavener, let's get that ankle to bed.'

'Don't expect me to be taken in by that kindly concern, Mr Tavener. I'll race you up the stairs.'

Chapter 2:
Side by Side

The White Horse was an old pub on the main road out of town, two small beamy parlours at the front, with a big extension at the back, made to look old; and beyond that, a garden stretching to the fields that climbed up to the chalk line of the downs. It was ideal for the morris, with a paved patio, no undulating grass to trip unwary ankles, and a children's playground with rigging to climb. There were dried hops over the bar, and a comfortable smell of beer and woodsmoke, even in summer. Jim, a laughing cavalier of a landlord, made the side welcome at least once a year. He didn't run to free beer but huge plates of sandwiches appeared after the stand.

Some of the side had arrived early and were savouring the local brew, an amber ale with a flowery lightness to its malt and hoppiness. Jim prided himself on keeping it in good condition.

'Can't beat a pint at lunchtime,' said Martin Tremayne. The side didn't have a Fool, but Martin, tall and thin with a gaunt face which hid his anarchic sense of fun, always appeared as a Gull. He was a reserved man, an accountant, not at all extrovert in his daily life, but once he was inside the Gull he was transformed. It was more of a second self to him, full of physical inventiveness.

Ray was watching the way the barmaid's blouse moved as she pulled pints.
'Cheers, Martin. You're right. As the song says:
"A pint when 'tis quiet, come lads let us try it,
For it's thinking will drive a man crazy." '

He raised his glass. 'Here's to Speed the Plough.'

'Not singing it, Ray?' said Martin with a serious face but a twinkle in his eye.

Lolly had got used to Ray's roving eye, but his flirtations seemed to her too obvious to be threatening. She was happy sitting with some of the women, chatting about how the new members of the side were coming along. It was a good thing foreman Alex couldn't hear some of the comments. Alex was always honest with himself about any weaknesses in the side's dancing, while being all-encouraging to people's faces. But he took it personally and got really shirty if other people criticised their dancing.

Brandon and Zoe breezed in a little late. No-one minded; it was a lovely day and Brandon was popular as squire. He went straight off to check that Jim was happy with the arrangements.

Zoe joined Lolly's corner table with some of the women. 'It's fun being married to a snail,' she said, raising her eyebrows.

'Put some salt on his tail then,' said Carol Murfin. She had a habit of leaning forward suddenly when she spoke. This jerked her straight brown hair out in two points, as if she was accusing anyone listening. 'On second thoughts, no, don't. Think of the slime.' The women's laughter was slightly awkward, as they were all accustomed to Zoe's tongue and Carol's sharpness, but they nearly all liked Brandon.

'Let's get this show on the road,' called Alex. 'Hankie first. It's The Quaker. Brisk Bampton stepping, lots of flourish in the chorus, please, and flick those wavers high.' He read out the chosen dancers. There was a general stir and out they went, into the shining afternoon. The fine weather had brought out a good crowd, grouped round the tables on the patio.

Lolly made her way over to Alex. 'I'm playing melodion these first two,' she said, 'but I think you said Step 'n' Fetch Her was third. Could I be in it as I'm also playing at the castle?' She only needed to keep half an eye for Naomi and Tamsin who were playing happily on the rigging with several other children. She felt quite daring, but people often canvassed Alex for positions, and he was flexible, provided a strong enough side was out for him to juggle names.

'Well, I had Sarah in there to keep young Luke company, but it'd be good to have an experienced dancer to support him.' A nervous Luke had only been voted in the month before.

'Thanks, Alex.' Lolly was so pleased she wondered whether to buy him a drink, but somehow that made his kindness into something a bit mercenary. She'd seen others do it blatantly, and he didn't always refuse, but the way he said 'experienced dancer' felt like an honest compliment. She felt appreciated.

The music lined up. Lolly with her small Castignari melodeon, Pete Kershaw on violin with his jerky movements but confident musicianship, and little Steve Tavener with his tambourine. He was a quiet eight-year-old, as blonde as his mother, and looked quite striking in his Larksea whites with a blue waistcoat. Being Hannah and Alex's son, he knew about keeping the beat, and on Pete's nod came in with a good clear tap. There was a gentle sigh amongst the six dancers standing to attention. The first lilting music of the stand was under way, and the familiar rhythm and release of the dance banished the niggling cares of the day.

Alex was calling this opening dance, and raising his waver high he called 'This time!' The audience quieted, some moving round to watch, drawn to the movement, the colour, and the distinctive jingling of the bells. All eyes were on Alex as the set faced the music. It was the sort of cheerful tune you wanted to whistle round the house, and with the little hop back of the once-to-yourself the whole side surged forward. Alex need not have worried. Twelve wavers did the neat double flick in white unison for the chorus. The side felt their hearts lift as the beat of the music kept their movements together, and they walked off the set with an aerobic glow of exhilaration. The audience could see a team of smiling faces and applauded loudly.

'Sticks now,' said Alex, circulating with the heavy canvas bag and handing sticks out to his chosen crew. He liked to alternate hankie and stick dances, and had never been a purist about changing traditions, knowing the public always responded to variety and the clash and vigour of the sticks. Balance the Straw in the Fieldtown tradition was a dance the side knew backwards, and a good loud clash of the sticks focussed everyone's attention. Last year a stick had shattered and a chunk of it had landed right in an old lady's glass of chardonnay. She had fallen off her chair in consternation. The memory of this incident did nothing to curb the exuberance of Ray's sticking. He was dancing opposite Carol now and the force of his blows made her palms tingle, but she gave as good as she got and made sure his hands were stinging as much as hers by the end of the dance.

Afterwards, Ray strolled over for a chat with Zoe in the bar. She was watching Alex doing the rounds to set up the following dance, but was eager to relay Carol's comment about Alex. 'It is funny, what she said,' grinned Ray. 'Looking at him now I can see all legs and no arse. But I still can't really connect a bit of Carol's bitchiness with our business on the beach the other night.'

'Well, maybe it was just a chance remark,' said Zoe. 'See if you pick up anything this afternoon. And look, Alex has gone to the others first. I think he's a bit apprehensive about approaching me. These things are subtle. Keep an eye out.'

Alex was irritated that he had to go into the bar to dig Zoe out when she knew she was in the next dance. 'Step'n'Fetch Her, Zoe,' he called from the door.

'Well he stepped and fetched *you*, I must say,' said Ray with a comic downturn of his mouth.

'I say *nerthing!*' Zoe quipped back.

During the dance one of the audience turned to have a bite of his sandwich and nearly jumped out of his skin. A huge gull had his beak on the plate. 'Here! Watchit!' he yelled and Gull squawked and flapped away, giving a little tweak to a woman's skirt as he passed. A couple of children ran up and tried to pull his tail, shrieking and dodging the clacking beak. Martin could see that a small child was afraid of this outlandish big bird and was actually whimpering, so Gull calmed things down by putting his head under his wing and letting the children stroke the wing feathers.

Alex was on the patio. 'Glad you're up for playing Step'n'Fetch Her, Len. Don't need to tell you to keep a steady beat.' Len Barnes was a stout, older man who took his music very seriously. He always watched the dancers' feet carefully so as not to play too fast and make them have to snatch at the movements.

'Good luck, Luke. Nice big surge in the cross capers, now.' Alex patted him on the shoulder. 'Must say your kit's looking really good. Shows up my tatty old blue ribbons.' Luke nodded and strode out with more confidence than he really felt. He was nineteen, handsome with his curly black hair, and not the youngest on the side; but the pressure of being the new boy made him nervous.

There was a strong side for this one. Brandon and Zoe were at the top; they always co-ordinated well. Hannah was opposite Johnny, who had an infectious smile and a witty way with words. Young Luke was at the bottom with Lolly, who was as nimble a dancer as she was a musician, unobtrusively matching her movements to whoever she was with. She had that instinctive feel for the way the whole dance could be affected by making good eye contact and watching closely.

Brandon didn't call 'This time.' Instead, he just turned his head slowly as if he was quelling a bunch of naughty children, and then nodded down the set. Everyone's hands and wavers were at their waists, and for a moment each dancer was absolutely still, then the whole set launched forward with the distinctive upward sweep of the Bampton style. Brandon was positively bouncing and he winked theatrically at Hannah in his first high caper. She responded with a quick flirtatious smile and a toss of her blonde hair as he returned to place.

'It's like that, is it?' thought Zoe, and in a moment's lapse of concentration almost collided with Luke who had taken Alex's words to heart and put everything into his first big caper. He relaxed; he'd done it! But he had a flicker of doubt – was he in the wrong position? Surely it wasn't Zoe's fault? He hesitated on the return, confronted her line, and veered to the left at the last minute, passing her on the wrong shoulder.

'Right shoulder, you idiot!' she hissed, and a very flustered Luke nearly turned the wrong way into the whole hey. He swerved but managed to recover.

Lolly made sure to give Luke a reassuring nod and mouthed 'ok,' as they passed in the half gyp. This time Brandon mimed a kiss at Hannah as he capered past her. It was not lost on Zoe and she gave him a contemptuous toss of the head as he returned. He was feeling too full of the joys not to feel defiant, so gave Hannah an extravagant kiss salute in the whole gyp. Hannah replied with a provocative mock-demure look. She saw Zoe looking daggers in the rounds, but passed it off to herself as intended for Luke. He was disconcerted, and though he didn't make any other obvious mistakes, his movement had become stiff and self-conscious.

Lolly noticed the exchanges but kept her smile. It was too good a dance, too nice a day, to let a pout of Zoe's spoil it, and the good-looking Brandon as your opposite corner was a partner to dance up to. The final salute felt very together.

They walked round and off the set. Luke made a point of saying 'Sorry, Zoe,' once they were out of the dancing area, but she ignored him.

'Don't worry, Luke.' Alex was right there with them. 'Tiny error, none of Jo Public noticed, they only watch the wavers. I'll put you in it again at the castle – and not with Zoe.' ''preciate it, Alex,' said Luke, and headed for the bar.

Ray walked up to Hannah and Lolly who were at the bar with Johnny. 'Pity about Luke,' he said, and took a swig at his beer.

Johnny looked him in the eye. 'Don't do your Ray-the-replay thing. It was a tiny wobble. The lad's doing fine. It looked fine. It certainly felt fine.' He glanced at Ray's empty pint. 'For a buzz, a good dance beats alcohol every time.'

Lolly nodded, but Ray persisted. 'Still, it's a pity when the rest of you are on such good form.'

'Don't be picky, darling.' Lolly wanted nothing to sour the mood. 'Now, what are you having?'

Gull had got his beak in someone's glass this time. He had grey gloves at his wingtips so could grasp it, and the pint's proprietor cheerfully joined in, so the beer sploshed as they fought over it. Gull's head moved in exaggerated jerks, just like a bird in a beach squabble. When he finally released the glass he pretended to sulk and drooped over to a bench to sympathetic murmurs. A woman actually offered him her drink.

'Brandon's in the dog house,' said Alex to Hannah at the bar afterwards. 'It's all your fault, you shameless hussy.' She feigned complete innocence. Alex just smiled.

But he would have to choose dancers very carefully at the castle now.

Chapter 3:
Dance Around

You could hardly call it a castle any more. There were just a few low walls with some niches, but the site at the top of the cliff made it seem as magical as Tintagel. The height gave the feeling of flying over the great expanse of glittering sea, and on a warm July day like this the breeze was sweet and tangy with salt. The grassy corners were perfect for picnics.

The craft fair had attracted a good crowd. Colourful clothes fluttered, jewellery gleamed, and the delicious smell of bacon from the mobile cafe all combined to make a holiday atmosphere. Children played with silver helium balloons covered in rainbow stripes which flashed in the sun.

Charlie Pritchard was acting as the bagman, chaffing the bystanders as he went round coaxing them to contribute to the collection pot. He was quite chubby but agile for man of fifty and he moved swiftly round the crowd,easily establishing a rapport with people. His experience as a jovial previous squire meant he had the right kind of style, and he went round now offering health, wealth and happiness in return for some goodwill and a few coins. The sunshine had thawed the usual English part-amused, part-embarrassed, part-curious response to the morris, and Charlie was doing rather well.

A young man approached Brandon to say it was his girlfriend's birthday, and could the side sing happy birthday and pose for a group photo with her.

'We can do better than that,' said Brandon, beaming with the afterglow of the lunchtime beer. 'Come with me and we'll set things up. What's her name?'

'Katie,' replied the boyfriend, pleased his plan for a little surprise was going so well. 'And I'm Barry. Thanks for doing this.'

Brandon strolled over to Alex. 'We've got a birthday girl,' he said. 'I think The Rose is in order, don't you?'

'Where is she?' asked Alex. 'Oh yes, pretty, as well. I'll get a set of the men up. The women can dance The Maid of the Mill later.' He went over to the unsuspecting girl.

'Hello, Katie, we've got something special for you.' He took her hand. She clearly felt awkward and looked round for her boyfriend, but she was suddenly surrounded by the men and some of the women. Alex doffed his hat and made a show of crowning her with it. The side grouped round. The Larksea kit looked good in the bright light, all whites with black top hats, blue rosettes on the shirts and blue ribbons at the elbow. The women had voted not to wear hats, but had ribbons or flowers in their hair. It made a striking photo with the girl in a top hat in the centre. The musicians struck up happy birthday and everyone sang, with none of the usual diffidence.

Katie thought the excitement was over, and made to return Alex's hat, but he took her hand again. 'We've got a special birthday dance for you,' he said as he led her protesting into the centre of a circle of six men, so she became the focus of the dance. She stood with her hands by her side, clutching her skirt. Lolly and Pete struck up the elegant music for The Rose, a mood shattered when the men stepped in to a tight circle and shouted 'Woof!' Katie let out a little shriek, but calmed down as the dancers performed a series of slow, upright jumps. Suddenly they did a big leap and were all round her, lifting her bodily up on to their shoulders.

'Barry!' she yelled, making desperate efforts to keep her skirt from riding up, but he was grinning and clapping with all the others gathered round. 'I'll get you for this!' she shouted above the applause.

Just as she regained her feet, Gull broke through the crowd and flapped around her, then wiggled backwards towards her, bottom first, produced a large white rubber egg from the seat of his trousers, and shoved it at her midriff. By now Katie was beyond embarrassment. She took the egg, swept off the top hat, and deposited it inside with a flourish.

Alex called out, 'That's a bit of morris luck for your birthday. Of course, once you've worn a morris man's hat, you'll get pregnant. The egg is proof!'

Katie smiled, but she wasn't safe yet. All six morris men came up to her, wished her happy birthday, and kissed her. She flushed with further embarrassment and a bit of pleasure. Even Barry now felt things had gone far enough, so firmly took her hand and kissed her.

'Thanks guys,' he called as he led her away.

Katie was suffused with relief now the ordeal was over. 'Yes, thanks! My birthday is getting quite interesting!' She waved mock graciously, forgiving them for the alarming surprise.

After Alex had reclaimed his hat, he walked over to the gents, but there was a queue. He knew you could climb over the wall further down if the warden wasn't looking, so strolled over. It really was a perfect day. He started counting the ships on the horizon. Eight. With a glance round, he vaulted over the wall – and nearly landed on a fox basking in the sun. Startled, it bounded away, leaving its sharp tang in the air. Alex's heart missed a beat. Then silence. It was as if the craft fair and the crowd were in another world. This was a completely other, older place he had stumbled into, rocks and brambles, flowers and insects, existing just outside consciousness, an alternative, indifferent to everyday concerns.
Alex breathed the quiet, warmed by the sun. He could hear the sighing of the sea, and lingered, not wanting to lose the wonder of the moment.

Back in the melee, the dancing had finished.

Hannah and Brandon were walking towards the beer tent. She tipped his hat forward. 'Well, Sir Brandon,' she teased, 'which of our merry maidens are you most pleased with this afternoon? Didn't Lolly dance well.'

'You were all mesmerising,' said Brandon gallantly. 'But no-one dips her garland as elegantly as you, Hannah.'

'That's what I like to hear. And I didn't even fish for the compliment. Your sincerity is coming along nicely,' she replied laughing. 'Don't let it go to your head, but you weren't so bad yourself.'

Zoe, standing by a pottery stall near the beer tent, noticed the exchange. She couldn't hear the words, but sensed the flirtation between them, and frowned.

Brandon strolled over to Lolly, thinking how well her short brown hair suited her neat figure. 'I've just been hearing compliments about your dancing,' he said. 'And the music's great. You really set a good tempo and don't speed up. It lets Pete do some nice slides and descants on the violin, too.'

'Things just feel good today,' sighed Lolly, colouring slightly. 'It's great when it all comes together.' She was too modest to tell him he made a really good squire, that it all worked better because he wasn't bossy but organised the stand so people knew where they were, and what to do, and they felt secure. Underneath the modesty, what was really stopping her from telling him was the pleasant but alarming zing she felt in his presence, this muscled man whose depth of good humour drew her, leaving her tongue-tied and slightly breathless.

Ray was also observing Brandon's bonhomie with his partner. He was relaxing by the beer tent with his crony Mike Tonkins, a dour sixty-year-old who hadn't voted for the side to go mixed. They frequently got into a huddle to pick away at individual personalities in the side.

'That Brandon's so bloody full of himself,' grumbled Ray. 'Like a cock strutting amongst his chickens.' He didn't have Brandon's natural style and attractiveness, and he knew it.

'Yes, he thinks he's the bees knees all right,' agreed Mike. 'The women all pander to him; he takes the blokes for granted. All clever and casual. He needs taking down a peg or two.' Mike felt envious, too. He wasn't as good a dancer as Brandon, either.

Ray sensed possibilities. 'Not all the women are gooey for him. We could sound a few people out before the AGM. And then get someone to tell him a few home truths, like his choice of stands has been pretty dodgy sometimes, and he's set on his favourite dances. Alex doesn't stand up to him, either. Long legged creep. Yeah, have a sniff round, Mike. I'll do the same.'

Zoe had a fresh air glow after the dancing, almost an aerobic high, but this didn't stop her casting about for all the little nuances she observed in the side's behaviour. Yes, I deserved my praise, she thought, and the side danced well. But there are compliments and compliments. Lolly's not going to get all pink with Brandon without my being in on it. She's sweet, she's lovely, not a bitchy bone in her body. Back off, Brandon. She felt a twinge of envy for Lolly's uncomplicated openness, and found herself being drawn towards her.

'Lolly, love, you were on top form today. The sun's brought out the best in you.'

Lolly mumbled her thanks. This was disconcerting; she never quite knew where Zoe was coming from.

'And you move beautifully. Oh, Lolly, I wish I was like you.' Zoe took her hand and stroked it, suddenly serious. 'I know I shouldn't say,but you're...' She pulled Lolly's hand up to her lips. 'I keep wanting to... watch you.' Zoe's eyes were wide and vulnerable.

Lolly's intake of breath was the only sign of her surprise. She didn't take her hand from Zoe's, but nor did she drop her gaze. There was a tense pause.

'There, oh dear, I can see I've troubled you. I just couldn't keep it in any longer. We are friends, aren't we?' Zoe's face was tender, pleading.

Lolly let out her breath. 'Um, yes, of course, you know we are,' she murmured.

'Oh, I knew you'd be kind. It was very hard for me to say. But I knew you'd understand...'

She was going to say something else, but to Lolly's relief Naomi and Tamsin were suddenly at her side with happy, animated faces. Zoe let go of her hand, and smiled. 'Can we talk later?'

'Oh, er, yes. 'Scuse us!' Lolly managed to say, as Noami tugged her away to a stall with garish plastic jewellery.

Lolly was preoccupied while Naomi and Tamsin kept pointing out florescent bracelets.

How odd. How embarrassing, she thought. I just don't trust her. But she could see that Zoe's earnest face and unmistakable emotion were bewilderingly real. I've no idea what to say to her. She's warm and forceful. And what else might she want to say to me? Where on earth do we go from here? Lolly was worried. And absent-mindedly paid for glowing beaded wristbands for Tamsin and Naomi, to their squeals of delight.

Ray had been about to go over to Lolly when with a twitch he saw Zoe holding her hand. What's that about? he wondered. Zoe would be aware that people could see her. Or was it just him? He was suspicious of this magnetic woman after the incident on the beach, but he openly admitted to himself how attractive he found her full, curvy figure and that long black hair. He turned and made his way over to her.

'Zoe, you delicious minx,' he teased.

'I'm sure I don't know what you mean.' She batted her eyelids theatrically at him. He was, after all, a well made man, quite broad shouldered, and those intense, lively blue eyes. Each knew they admired each other, and thought they understood each other, too. Ray met her eyes. The thought, go carefully here, flashed through his mind, and he leant forward conspiratorially.

'Some news on the Chinese whispers front,' he said, lowering his voice. 'People excuse Alex, don't mind him much, but I thought you ought to know I've picked up some comments about Brandon.'

'I'm sure you're going to tell me.' Zoe inclined her head towards him.

'Well, I know he's your fella and all, but some people are finding him a bit over the top. That cheeky chappie stuff he uses to get people to go along with him – it's causing some resentment. Not today of course, but they say his choice of stands hasn't always been brilliant.'

'Oh, I've told him that. But you think the little rumblings we've directed at Alex aren't as productive as a few barbs about Brandy? And who's said what?'

'Mike's got a thing or two to say, and he was surprised to hear Charlie agreeing with him.'

'Not much to go on. I should have thought Brandon was pretty unassailable as squire.' Zoe was thinking quickly. 'We've talked about it. He'd be happy to do another year. I don't really want him to – it's such a tie. I don't mind if you start a hare or two. You're not likely to get to him.'

'Ve must see vot ve can do.'

A weaselly thought came into Ray's mind. He just grinned at Zoe. A distinct current passed between them, and they left it at that, but his mind was racing. He wondered if he could get a rumour going that Brandon was having an affair with Hannah, and he was intrigued to see how this might affect Zoe.

Autumn

Autumn

Chapter 4:
Sidesteps

September, and the schools went back; a welcome return to routine for some, the closing down of bright summer for others. For the morris, it was morris on.

The side had a local ploughing match to look forward to, a favourite autumn booking, one of those stands that felt right, part of beating the boundaries of your own patch, and a link to the past after harvest.

*

On practice nights, Ray had not been idle at the rumour factory. Perhaps it was because a few of the women would have quite liked to believe there was something more to Brandon's flirtatious manner. It was a bit of fun to fantasize that there might be room for more than one on board. Ray guessed which of them might take it more seriously, and he had been careful in choosing whose fantasy he could fertilise first. Carol Murfin was not noticeably a gossip, but she often complained about her husband Colin, life in general, and some members of the side in particular. She readily jumped to the conclusion that it was Hannah who was the subject of Ray's hints. The rumour wasn't spreading like wildfire, but she told Ray she'd found echoes in a couple of the women.

At the practice before the ploughing match there was a good turn-out, with a double set up for Shepherd's Hey Bampton, and everyone liking the idea of both sets breaking into a large round for the final figure. The old scout hall where they practised was roomy, if spartan, with that musty school-like smell of other people's clothes. Feet on the wooden floorboards made a rhythmic thudding as loud as drums, but stick dances in the cavernous space reverberated like muffled gunfire.

Carol was doing her rounds, and approached Lolly at the back of the hall. After a little polite chat, she suddenly leant forward, hair jutting, and said quietly, 'Have you watched Brandon and Hannah recently? Do you think...well, there's something, you know, going on between them? I think they've got a thing for each other.'

'No, really?' Lolly pretended surprise, but couldn't take Carol seriously. To her, both Brandon and Hannah were in stable relationships. A few signs of tension were just par for the course.

Lolly sat down on one of the small hard chairs scattered round the hall. As Carol moved away, Zoe approached in her new friendly way, and sat down beside her.

'God these little chairs are uncomfortable. It's like being sent to the naughty girls' corner!' Zoe grinned, and Lolly smiled back, feeling a little mistrustful, though there had been no direct repeat of the challenging conversation at the castle that had made her feel so self-conscious. But Zoe was so genuinely warm, and it was impossible not to bask a little in someone else's admiration.

'I've been watching young Angie,' said Zoe. 'She's got Hannah's ease. She may be only twelve, but her stepping's already as good as some I could mention. Sickening how quick some adolescents can be.'

'I wish Naomi was drawn to the dancing. She's sporty and agile, but somewhere she's caught a bit of the morris-is-a-joke attitude. We always have to get a babysitter on practice nights.'

'Well I can't offer practice nights, of course,' said Zoe, 'but I'd be happy to babysit for you occasionally. I like Naomi. She says what she thinks. And to be honest I wouldn't mind getting out of the house for a quiet evening from time to time.'

And I wouldn't mind getting out of mine sometimes, too, thought Lolly. She had come to be very fond of Naomi, but the domestic routine imposed by someone else's child – well, I'm not a goddess, she grinned to herself, and gave Zoe a smile. 'I'd have to ask Ray, of course,' but she knew he'd agree.

'Uh oh,' said Zoe. 'His master's voice.' She plucked at Lolly's sleeve. 'Looks like we've been called.'

They got up together to join the whole side in a big circle. Alex was demonstrating Fieldtown stepping and drilling everyone into standing straight and taking deep breaths, allowing the wavers to float down gracefully.

Later, back in their orderly modern maisonette, Ray did agree. Enthusiastically. 'Great. We've missed several good films over the summer, and a mid week break every so often... yes, and someone we know and can trust... I don't suppose she'll ask for money, either.'

Lolly had little inkling that Ray was tickled by the prospect of having more opportunities to see Zoe. He immediately thought of offering to pick her up and take her home, twenty minutes just-to-themselves. Her thoughts were more about Carol's rumour. She wouldn't dream of mentioning it to Zoe; it would be very much up to Zoe to open the subject if she wanted to. Besides, she continued to feel dismissive of the gossip, even if Zoe appeared to want to escape from home every so often. The trouble was it was so easy to read things into other people's behaviour. A little harmless banter could suddenly seem threatening or sinister.
'Pardon, love?' She wasn't concentrating on what Ray was saying.

'Zoe'd be a good babysitter. I could always offer to pick her up, couldn't I?' Lolly thought he was being helpful.

*

Neither Hannah nor Alex were aware of the whispers. Hannah had been particularly focussed on the dancing at practice that evening, as she and Alex were having an on-going discussion about whether she should stand as the next foreman. She had taken practice a few times when Alex was away, and enjoyed it. Now they were going over the ground again, relaxing on their large, comfy old sofa with a last cuppa.

'I haven't run out of steam, not really,' said Alex. 'You know what I'd really like to do is introduce Sherbourne. We do Monk's March pretty well with the right set, but think of those high galleys and all those glorious tunes! Orange in Bloom, Lads-a-Bunchum....'

'I know. But it's a huge change. You'd need a couple of years at least to get it fully established, and in some ways we're still adjusting to being a mixed side. What we've got is good Bampton and some reasonable Fieldtown, plus some popular leftovers from the old days, like Adderbury Shooting.' She leaned forward, eyes bright as she warmed to her theme. 'I really do think we should just develop Fieldtown. We can add things like Mrs Casey as a heel-and-toe, and it would be fun to do a column dance like Banks of the Dee. When Mum can't babysit you could bring the kids to practice and leave at half time. It's not as if we live far away. Angie would enjoy going more often, and Steve would love being out with you and picking up some more music. You've done it for two years, you said it would be nice to have a break. Go on, let me have a turn. You'll be there to be the back seat driver if I hesitate. I bet you couldn't resist throwing in your pennyworth.'

Alex grinned. He always loved her enthuisiasm. 'Oh, bugger it. Goodbye, Orange in Bloom! But it's true, I'd be glad not to have the hassle next year. And the kids... maybe they could come. Your mum's very good with them, I'm sure she would be flexible. Okay, Mrs Foreman, have a go.'

'Great. I know who'll propose and second me for the AGM in a couple of weeks. Wouldn't do for you to nominate me – nepotism in the family and all that. Back to swotting up in the Black Book for me! And thanks, love. I know how much it's meant to you. You've really brought the less enthusiastic ones into all the dances. And if I get it, there'll be continuity as I'll be building on what you'e done already.'

*

It had not occurred to them that others might actually be interested in the job of foreman. Zoe was secretly toying with the idea. Her spontaneous offer to babysit for Lolly, but definitely not on practice nights, made her realise she really would like a crack at foreman. Sitting in a corner of the scout hall, water bottle in hand, she watched Alex enviously.

Hm. Me, Zoe The Foreman, she thought. The women pleased to have someone who understands things from their point of view, the men in reluctant admiration. Not that I'm likely to get it, but hey, let's get it in the open and see what happens.

As soon as they got home, she quickly made mugs of coffee and went into the large living room of their spacious flat. Drawing the curtains on the high windows, she said casually: 'AGM soon, Brandy. Are you sure you want to stand as squire again?'

'I'm certainly thinking about it.' Brandon sprawled in his favourite black leather armchair. 'I feel I've got the hang of it, and I wanted to make sure everyone felt included. Charlie was sometimes a bit cliquey when he was squire, you know, always sticking to the same stands, same dances, same people in them. Now I think most people have a sense of being able to turn their hands to the whole repertoire, and I want to continue that. Good old Alex. Yes, I'll stand.'

And enjoy the attention, thought Zoe, piqued at his warmth for Alex.

'Ok. But...' She hesitated. 'I've been thinking, well, what would you say if I stood for foreman?' No initial response from Brandon. 'I've been mulling it over. It's true you've brought everyone in as far as possible, but I think a woman foreman would move the side on. I'd like to work on the women's sticking, and we dance Bampton – let alone Adderbury – too fast. The men are quite strong and Alex has done what he can with the women, but I think a female foreman would bring our whole style together.'

'Blimey, Zoe, you're a dark horse.' Brandon sat up abruptly. 'I took it for granted Alex would go on. It's not a job many people want. Only trouble could be if the side thought the two of us had too much sway. Alex jokes about the burdens of responsibility, but I guess he's half sincere in not wanting a third year. Yes,' he chuckled, 'I like the idea. Go for it, girl.'

'Thanks! Good – oh. I'll just make another coffee. I want to talk more about this.'

Zoe retired to the kitchen, in truth thrown into turmoil by Brandon's unexpectedly positive reaction. She started to rinse the mugs, staring at the bright abstract designs, and found herself plunged into a bout of self-accusation. She longed for the kind of underlying respect that Alex had, but faced with the possible reality of the job, her self doubt drained all her confidence.
Her thoughts ran on: what's wrong with me? Things don't ever work out quite as I want them. I don't seem to achieve anything long term. Always a bit of emptiness underneath. Oh, stop it, bloody self pity.

She rubbed at a stain on the mugs with unnecessary vigour. The kettle boiled and steamed.

I have lots of satisfactions. Reasonable mortgage on this flat, career, yes. Sex. The dancing. But it's all precarious, all so temporary. Men direct their lives, get what they want. Why can't I? Do men have more self respect, more selfishness? Even in love. Always their bit of lust left over. Maybe a woman can give love, real care, instinctive understanding, real selfless love....
She swept her hair back from her face, tried to push her inner anguish aside, and carried the coffee back into the living room. Brandon looked up, smiling.

Zoe gulped. 'I feel sort of fuzzy, darling, half worried, half excited. How about a gin and tonic?'

Brandon readily agreed, pleased to feel something vulnerable but warm and positive in Zoe's manner. He kissed her and went to the drinks cupboard.

*

The prospect of the AGM was exercising Ray, too. He'd had a frustrating week, not being able to concentrate on writing the blurbs for the houses that had just come onto the estate agents' books. Normally he was good at it, a balancing act between pleasing the client and avoiding a style that was too effusive. He was quite proud of his ability to serve both sides simultaneously, with enough cynicism to exploit things to his advantage. He felt Zoe was someone else who could see through people. Between them, he thought, they could have a bit of a field day at this AGM.

So, in the pub with others from the side playing darts later that weeek, he told Zoe what he had gleaned about the criticisms of Brandon, but not that Carol had taken his bait about the possible affair between him and Hannah. The hubbub of chatter in the pub made a good cover for conversation. He was almost thrown by her reaction.

'Why don't you stand as squire yourself? You're a good organiser. Brandon's been popular but from what you say, quite a few think he's too laissez-faire. He's going to stand, but I'm not really sure I want him to because...' She put her head on one side. 'Can I tell you something in confidence? I'm going to canvass to be foreman. I've talked to Brandon about it, but he's the only one so far. A new squire and a new foreman would give as all fresh energy. I know I can get some support amongst the women, but I need some of the men to be adventurous about a woman foreman. Could you gently spread the word and support me? And if you were squire, what a pair we'd make. We could really take the side forward.'

'It hadn't even occurred to me.' Though not quite true, Ray did rather like the idea. Images of himself as squire flashed through his mind. Ray the skilled leader, firm but diplomatic; people's surprise and admiration at his success. Oh yes.

'I'll have to think about it.'

He began humming to himself, plans forming as he half listened to Zoe talking through her ideas.

*

The day of the Ploughing Match dawned grey and wet. The side weren't due to dance till teatime, after the main competitions, and by then the clouds had cleared. The late September afternoon was tinged with gold in the level autumn light. Even the huge tractors looked elegant, with their ploughshares flashing and gulls wheeling round. There were duckboards over the damp, sweet smelling grass, and they made a comfortable squelching sound as shoes and wellingtons pressed them down into the soft earth.

Between the refreshments tent and the main marquee an area was boarded. It made an attractive arena for the morris. There had been a children's entertainer earlier, and despite the soggy bunting there was a pervasive mood of relaxed good humour.

As the side gathered in this mellow atmosphere, Ray was discussing the past year with Charlie. They sipped from their tankards, taking in the distant view of the downs and watching people go by. Ray started to hold forth.

'Brandon's been fine as squire but the side need galvanising. Things like a good foreign trip, respond to a couple of invitations to other sides' Ales.... It's good that we've got a mixture, a spread of ages, but we're getting a bit bogged down with family concerns. It'd really put us on our mettle to get away a few times – like we did when you were squire – meet other sides more, that sort of thing.'

Charlie shrugged his thickset shoulders and pulled a wry face. 'Hm. Am I hearing a bit of canvassing about whether I'd stand? The answer is no. But am I hearing an interest in doing the job yourself? I'd be prepared to nominate you. It's good to have a proper election, otherwise I guess Brandon will walk it and think everyone agrees with him.'

'Thanks, Charlie. Well, yes, I'd rather like to have a go. But you know, people would take you seriously because of your experience. I'm not trying to be clever, but if people got used to the idea of there being someone else besides Brandon who's prepared to stand, do you think you could let me propose you, but then you withdraw and support me? I can see you're really not keen to be squire again yourself, but if you spoke in my favour, it would really count for something.'

'You devious old bastard!' laughed Charlie. 'A kind of stalking horse, you mean? As I said, I certainly don't want to be squire again. Well, it's just a bit of a laugh. No harm in it I suppose. People will make their own minds up anyway.'

Suddenly, any thoughts of machinations melted from their minds. The stand was underway, and the light was fading; a set was up for Dearest Dickie, and as the graceful old melody unfurled, the dancers stood perfectly still. The dusk light was a kind of hazy blue, almost violet, and the side's white trousers and shirts glowed, as if they were lit from within. Blue waistcoats and ribbons were scarcely visible, even faces were dimmed, but suddenly the wavers flicked high and flowed down, all together, twelve twisting columns of iridescent white.

Alex stood watching, a bittersweet pint in his hand, savouring the beer and the magic of the moment, proud of the morris. That's why we do it, he thought. It's as English as Greensleeves: there's nothing else like it; it's our dance.

Chapter 5:
Whole Gyp

After the ploughing match, there was only one practice before the Annual General Meeting. There was more of a buzz than usual, partly because the stand had gone so well, and partly because nominations for officers were due in. At the end of the evening, Brandon announced that he and Charlie were standing for squire; Hannah and Zoe for foreman. This caused a stir, as many had expected Alex to continue.

*

The scout hall stood silent and unlit the following week. A blustery wind with a strong tang of salt blew nearly thirty of the side, a few more women than men, into the back room of The Anchor. Till everyone sat down, it was shoulder to shoulder at first round the cramped square of tables set for the meeting.

Brandon hadn't produced an agenda. He relied on Carol to read the minutes, and simply followed the same pattern. So, first on the non-agenda, officers' reports: mostly pats on the back all round. Thanks were proposed, seconded, passed, and applauded: so far so good.

Charlie cleared his throat. 'While I've still got my hands on the money, I propose a drink on the bag. Can't have my successor thinking we're flush!' The motion was enthusiastically seconded from several quarters, and proceedings were suspended while the drinks were brought in.

'Now, election of officers,' called Brandon. There was an expectant hush. 'As you know, Charlie and I are standing. I don't want to say a lot. I think we've had a good year. We've found our feet (ho ho) as a mixed side with a good balance of stands, and if I'm squire I'd like to continue in the same way, making sure everyone has a go. That's all, really.'

Some 'here heres' round the room. All eyes were now on Charlie.
'It's no good Brandon. It simply won't do.'

It was suddenly very quiet in the room. Charlie looked round. 'We can't continue under a squire who LOST Roy the Rover.'

Relief, followed by laughter. The side's mascot was a spotty felt dog with bendy legs and a marked propensity to attach itself to people's lower parts in doggy fashion.

'The mail has delivered cries of help from our Roy. He has been abducted by an unmentionable local side and sent to foreign climes. Please pass round these two photographs that prove how serious the situation has become.' Rover on the parapet of a bridge in Paris looking at the Eiffel Tower; Rover in sunglasses on a towel with his little paws stretched behind his head.

As the photos started to circulate, Martin stood up, looking rather gaunt and not at all in his Gull role. 'Through the chair I should like to propose Roy as squire. He clearly needs all our support.' This was loudly seconded by Biff, a potential rival to Martin as a clown.

A hand shot in the air. 'You can't do that, Mr Chairman. It's unconstitutional. Nominations have to be in before the meeting opens.' It was Mike Tonkins, only half joking.
Brandon was enjoying the free-for-all. 'Martin, you are clearly Rover's proper representative. Can you defend his very late decision to lift his leg in the election?'

'Yes, certainly. The poor chap couldn't even be here! Charlie is clearly concealing Roy's official application and all the careful notes he sent about what he'd like to do. I put it to you, Charlie is just envious of Rover and won't let his little bark be heard arf arf.'

'Lies!' called Charlie. 'He hasn't woofed a word. But seriously everyone, I stood for squire because it's always good to have a fair election rather than just someone getting it by default, so to speak, however good they are. I've thought about things during the week, and I realise I've too many commitments. I don't want the responsibility this year. So as Roy can't do it, I propose Ray.' The surprise in the room was palpable. 'It's only a change of vowel, after all,' he added with a wry grin.

Brandon shook his head a little, as if to clear it. 'Are you sure about this?' Charlie nodded strongly.

'Ray, is this okay with you?'

'I'd like to second Charlie's proposal,' put in Phil Clothier quickly. He was one of the more conservative members of the side. 'I've spoken to Ray and I think we should consider what he has to say.'

'But this really is unconstitutional!' Mike exclaimed. 'You can't just make it up as you go along.' Ray was surprised at Mike's vehemence. He thought Mike would have been more interested in upsetting the apple cart by ousting Brandon, rather than getting excited about the nuts and bolts of procedure.

'What do people think?' Brandon looked bemused. Mostly nods and murmurs of 'let's hear him.'

'Brandon, I don't want to betray any confidences.' Eyes swivelled to Zoe. 'But as your partner, I know you're not one to complain, and people should know that you're often worried about being squire and you've wondered about giving it up this year, though you came round to it recently. We all know you've done a good job of representing the side, you're a good front man, but I rather think you wouldn't mind standing down. I should like to propose Hannah.'

'Oh no!' Hannah was taken aback. 'I'm up for foreman. But not squire. I haven't thought about it.'

'But you'd be a really good choice.' Zoe was intense. 'We've seen you organise several events and you always stay calm, you're fair to everyone, and you have strong thoughts about the way the side can develop. Please accept.'

Hm, thought Carol. Interesting. Is Zoe trying to get at Brandon? Maybe embarrassing Hannah by pushing her into his role, making some tension between them? She raised her eyebrows at Amy, sitting next to her, who was usually sympathetic

Phil and a few of the older members wondered if Zoe was playing the gender card, wanting a woman in the central role. Zoe's proposal echoed some of the old dilemmas about whether the side should go fully mixed in all respects. Their speculations were given a bit of substance when several of the women, including Carol and Amy, enthusiastically supported the idea of Hannah as squire.

Ray thought Zoe was being clever, weakening Brandon's chances. If Hannah stood, as well as him and Brandon, she could split the vote, and his own case would be stronger.

The people who obviously liked the thought of Hannah as squire, both men and women, were mostly the ones she knew would have voted for her as foreman. Suddenly she wasn't sure.

'Brandon, can I have a word with Alex? This is all a bit new.'

'Yes, of course. Five minutes break, everyone.' There were a few mutterings as people shifted in their seats.

Alex brought a large white wine over to Hannah in the corner of the bar.

'Well, this is interesting. You've got some real support. Do you want to consider it, seriously?' He was surprised, but drawn into the drama of the turnabout, pleased by the vote of confidence in his wife.

'It depends on you, really.' Hannah was earnest. 'I know you made a bit of a sacrifice when you agreed to let me stand as foreman. If you would like to do it for another year, then yes, I'm sort of excited. I'd like to be squire. More networking with other sides. Yes.'

Alex nodded. 'You pretty well convinced me we should follow the Fieldtown path, and not try to introduce a tradition as new to us as Sherbourne. Maybe start it gently, but there's so much good Fieldtown, so I'd go on with that.'

'I probably won't get squire. A three way fight and all that. But I really don't want Ray as squire. He's too manipulative, and he can be confrontational. Brandon didn't look surprised or upset. Maybe Zoe's right, and he's reluctant.

He'll probably get it anyway. But I'm warming to it now. Who'll propose you?'

'I'll just throw it open to the floor. Blimey, if people aren't prepared to propose me off the cuff, there's no point in standing.'

'Okay. Well, here we go then!'

Several members of the side patted her shoulder as she re-entered the room. Animated conversations dried. Hannah cleared her throat.

'Well everyone, you know I was up for foreman. Some of what I wanted to do with the dancing can carry over to the squire's role, like keeping everyone aware of the need to project the enjoyment of the morris. We need to turn those frowns of concentration into eye contact and smiles!' There were grins and a scattering of applause. Hannah felt encouraged. 'Obviously I haven't worked on lots of detail, but I've had conversations with some of you where we've talked about trying to make more links with other sides, more shared stands and so on. A bit of rivalry on a stand brings out the best in us. That's my main plan. Oh, and to vote newcomers in as soon as the foreman thinks they're ready, not have the whole side voting and maybe discouraging people. We lost a couple of potential members that way.'

Her initial surge of words trailed away, as a sudden awkwardness at all the attention came over her.

Brandon nodded. 'Good. Thanks, Hannah. Ray, it's your turn.'

Ray decided not to stand up, but spread his arms out to look authoritative. He pitched straight in.

'We need to be much more proactive. We could promote ourselves much more effectively, and bring in more paid stands. Then we'd be able to subsidise aways to Ales and a trip abroad. Those people from Le Touquet were pretty keen to have us, and we can exploit our twin town link. We could probably get more support from the Council, too. I'd like to see a full programme published in April so people know where they are. There's been quite a lot of shilly-shallying this year, last minute scrambles. We lost a couple of good bookings by playing safe with little local stands. We're strong enough with the combined men and women to be more outgoing now. I want to see us build on the good name we're getting.'

Had he sounded a bit more negative than he'd meant? No, it was strong and reasonable, he thought. He didn't hear someone mutter, 'Who does he think we are? Hammersmith?'

Brandon pulled a face and nodded. 'Okay, thanks Ray. Well, in the light of what you say, and as Hannah is prepared to stand, I'm going to withdraw. Make it a good clean fight between the two of you.'

There were a couple of calls of 'Don't!' and 'Hang in there, Brandon!' but a few more firm but friendly remarks made it clear he meant it. Carol passed round the slips for voting.

The atmosphere was tense, with sideways glances and much careful folding of paper. Silence as Carol counted the slips. She looked up.

'Ray nine, Hannah nineteen.'

Brandon was on his feet straight away. 'Congratulations, Hannah! I'm sure we'll all pull together to support you. Bad luck, Ray. Glad you were prepared to stand. Over to you, Hannah.'

'Well done, Hannah!' This from Zoe, who started clapping. Most joined in.
Hannah looked flushed. 'Thanks, everyone. Brandon, you did a really good job. Hope I can do as well.' Emotions were running high in the crowded room.

'Right! On to the election of foreman. Obviously I can't be foreman as well, but as you gather I spoke to Alex in the break, and he's prepared to stand again after all. Can we have a proposer?'

Johnny Rendell jumped in. 'Can we? You betcha. You must be joking. Yes, certainly.' Quickly seconded.

Hannah felt relieved. 'We've got a straight contest then. Zoe, would you like to outline your ideas first?'

Mike cut in, glaring at Hannah. 'Through the chair, I have to say again that this is all wrong. What's the point of having a constitution if you ignore it? We're snatching decisions out of the air here.'

Hannah knew this was her first test. 'Mike, I know it's dear to you, and you spent a lot of time two years ago setting our constitution up. It's a really helpful guide. But we're just a group of people with a strong shared interest, and surely we can be flexible. It feels as if what we're doing now reflects 'the mood of the meeting,' ' the will of the side' and so on. Is that okay with everyone?'

There were lots of nods and murmurs of agreement in the cramped room.

Zoe was thrown. Against Hannah, she had stood a chance. Against Alex, her experience looked thin. She tried to muster a confident manner, and stood up.

'This is it then. As some of you know, my main worry has been that we dance Bampton much too fast. It can look, well, comical. I'd like to concentrate on bringing out a Bampton style of our own, and introduce some new dances. The public particularly like stick dances, and I want to work on the women's sticking and bring in Sweet Jenny Jones and the Bluebells of Scotland.' There was more than polite interest. You could see people turning this over in their minds. 'The double time sticking at the end really goes down well but it must be very together. Also, I'm proud we're a mixed side now, but that's no reason a few separate dances can't go on. The men do a good job on The Rose; I'd like to see the women do The Maid of the Mill with coloured wavers.'

She sat down quickly, feeling breathless.

Alex nodded, with a genuine acknowledgement of Zoe's ideas.

'I could pinch some of that, Zoe!' he grinned. 'But you know me. I'm pleased with our Bampton, no reason to put that on the back burner when we're out, and it's nice and approachable for all those new recruits we hope we're going to get. No, it's Fieldtown that I want to develop. I've thought of Sherbourne, love it, but we've already got a good base in Fieldtown, and if Bampton's rich, Fieldtown's sumptuous. Dearest Dickie at the ploughing match had them entranced. That's me!'

They went straight to the vote. Zoe seven, Alex twenty-one.

Hannah immediately said, warmly. 'You've given us some options and things to think about. Thanks for standing, Zoe.'

This was all too much for Mike.

'May I point out through the chair that what we've done is NOT elect a single one of the officers who were properly nominated. No time to consider. All done in a rush. I wish to register my strong objection.' And he walked out.

Charlie got up too. Hannah was very alarmed. It would be awful if two men walked out just as she was starting her watch.

'Now I'm a happy un-squire, I'd be a happy bagman again. To persuade you all not to bother with an election, I propose another drink on the bag!'

A loud squawk, a sharp gull 'kree harr!' from Martin. 'It's unconstitutional!' he shouted.

The tension dissolved in merriment. Amid guffaws of laughter, the planned discussion about next year's programme looked like a very moveable feast, and the meeting broke up as the side collapsed cheerfully into the bar.

Chapter 6:
Stamp and Caper

'A good night's work there, Mr Not-squire.' It was Claire Rendell at the practice after the AGM. She had wanted Brandon as squire, but supported Hannah in the election.

'Win some, lose some,' replied Ray. After ten years of being an estate agent, a few barbed remarks were like water off a duck's back to him. He was more irritated than angry at the way things had gone. So much for Zoe's spells, he thought, with Alex decisively re-elected as foreman. But his confidence wasn't dented by his own defeat; he was enough of a realist to know the odds were against him. Besides, there had been some benefit, as Phil Clothier had supported him, and that meant he was in with the small caucus of older men who were still uncomfortable with the change to a mixed side. So he had his corner, and an apology to Mike about the irregular way he had stood for squire brought him back as a crony. And now Hannah was squire, he started to wonder how he could add to the rumour he'd started, and wind her up to vent his frustrations.

If Ray could be philosophical about the situation, Zoe was troubled. She thought she'd made a good speech, and a bit of her was pleased to have thrown her hat into the ring. But her envy of Alex deepened. It didn't reassure her that Carol and a couple of others had been sympathetic, and Lolly had been kind, too, though she hadn't voted for her. They were still perfectly happy to work with Alex, and she told herself that their support was just friendliness, not respect for her. A more fluttering concern was that Brandon had merely shrugged when she'd asked him if he'd minded her proposing Hannah, and there had been no relaxed pillow talk to be sure of his real feelings.

At times like this, when she was thrown back on herself, Zoe often turned to the I Ching to see if it gave her a picture of her situation. Several days after the AGM, she waited for Brandon to go out for a parents' evening, and got out the little book she used to interpret the hexagrams. Settling herself at the dining room table, she warmed the three old copper coins she used for casting the pattern, and began to think of the question she wanted to ask the oracle. I want a picture of where I'm going now, she thought, but rejected this as too general. Be clear, be more specific, she told herself. Her concerns at the moment were mostly with the morris; so that was it. it. She focussed her mind on the question: what does the future hold for me in the morris? and started to cast the coins.

Heads counted as three, tails two. Six throws. This gave her a score of 38, the number for the hexagram K'uei, entitled Neutrality and Disunity. Her heart sank. The picture of a flame leaping up, but a cold lake below, meant conflict, she knew. The printed commentary said her circumstances were stagnant. Well that's true, she thought, and read on: 'A wise person should not let temporary moods affect them. When isolated or in conflict, be more generous to others, but always be yourself.'

More generous to others in the morris? Lolly sprang to her mind. And she winced at the thought that her ill-will towards Alex had rebounded on her. Always herself? That was a tricky one if you often found you weren't certain of yourself. Getting guidance was the whole purpose of consulting the oracle! She sighed, and chinked the coins in her hand. What else does the hexagram say?

'The cart is halted, and the oxen dragged to a standstill.'
Quaint, these old poetic images, she thought, but that makes sense. I do feel I'm in the doldrums. What next?

'A time of complex, even dangerous obstacles will be followed by harmony.' And a last line: 'Danger continues. You meet a strong man of the same goodwill.' Could that be Brandon? No, she felt she had to move outwards to meet this person. Ray was confident, they shared the same sort of aspirations. Yes. It must be him.

There were three changing lines in the hexagram, giving a new score and so a new picture. This turned out to be number 18, Ku, and the commentary said: 'Make good what has been ruined. The wind tears at the foot of the mountain, which suggests negative or incompatible arrangements.'

This part must be about Brandon, she thought. My future in the morris is so bound up with his. Incompatible arrangements? Many little doubts and niggles came back to her. Only the other day they had had a row about which film to go to, and he'd accused her of being an intellectual snob, unable to enjoy a good story if it wasn't cultured in her terms. That still rankled, partly because she did think he could be a bit common at times.

Now the last image: 'There is benefit in crossing the water.' This must be a metaphor for a new journey, reinforced by the comment 'time to take decisive action to repair the damage done.'

She got up, hugging herself, and walked through to the living room, staring vacantly out of the big window. It's never as clear as you'd like, she thought, but what have I got from this reading? Be generous. I'll try to be supportive of Alex, and nice to Lolly. I need to meet a strong man. That's a bit gypsy fortuneteller-ish. She paused. Doubts swirled in her mind, but she wanted to believe, and dismissed an urge to mock the arcane images.

She nodded to herself. Yes, it's indicating Ray. The problem is, what should my decisive action be? It's all very well saying harmony will follow, but it won't if I take the wrong decisive action. 'The wind tears at the foot of the mountain.' Is the mountain my relationship with Brandon? I must sleep on this, let my mind settle.

She carefully put the I Ching away. The image of a high wind buffeting her as she struggled along stayed with her.

*

A couple of weeks after the AGM, Ray went to fetch Zoe to babysit.

'Almighty bloody Taveners,' exclaimed Ray. 'They've got it all now, and much good may it do them. I must say I hadn't for a moment seen the likelihood of Brandon withdrawing. You didn't say anything.'

'Once Charlie withdrew, I felt you'd stand a better chance if I divided the vote further. I didn't think Brandon would suddenly withdraw.'

'Thanks, anyway. It was a clever manoevre. Well, we'll just have to see what happens.'

'Now Alex is back, there's no point in opposing him, is there? We might as well be supportive. Others can think we're being good sports, but you and I can be friends in adversity.'

Ray nodded, amused at Zoe's change of tack. He said nothing about the progress of his Hannah and Brandon rumour.

Zoe was just settling in to Ray and Lolly's bright IKEA sitting room, when Naomi, who attended the primary section of Maywood School, started chatting about some of the staff. Zoe was not above listening to Naomi's opinions and drawing her out about school gossip. Naomi was also full of plans for her tenth birthday party.

'We're going to go to Brighton to the big leisure pool that's got the giant flumes. It'll be awesome! I'm just taking a few of my friends. And Lolly's booked this special home-made burger restaurant afterwards. We've got our own room and everything!'

'She's a good mum, isn't she? Not bossy like me. She's kind, and listens. I like her so much. She always looks good too, don't you think? I expect she helps you with choosing clothes and...' Naomi, with the acuity of a nine-year-old, picked up immediately on Zoe's ingratiating tone. She cut her off.

'Yes, I can talk to Lolly more than my real mum. When I visit Jacqui she's always on at me, do this, do that, and I don't think she really likes me. Or the way I look. But she's ever so glamorous.' Naomi sighed.

'You've got a good figure now with all your swimming and sports. I'm sure you can be as glamorous as her later.'

'But I've got spots! It's horrible. You don't know what it's like, people looking at you. And I'm not in the top set for anything. At least Tamsin's got her recorder, and does concerts and stuff.'

Zoe tried to be soothing, but Naomi remained bristly. They chose a dvd, and Zoe let her stay up well past her bedtime.

Next morning Naomi was in a sunnier mood. 'Zoe's all right, isn't she, Mum?' she said as she crunched her toast. 'She likes you. Thinks you're kind and always look good.'

'Really? Well, that's nice.' Lolly changed the conversation.

*

Bonfire Night was approaching. The town always had a lively procession, ending with a huge bonfire on the beach and fireworks from the castle. Most of the side had carried torches last year, but it had inhibited the dancing, quite apart from the occasional whiff of singed hair. At the meeting after practice one night they decided to do the Winster processional this year. Luke wanted everyone to use black wavers, maybe black their faces.

'We can't just float about looking summery. We need something to mark the fact that it's Samhain and dark and winter. It'll look strong and dramatic.'

'You'll lose the effect of the wavers, though, in the night. And I don't want black face paint on my kit.' Claire Rendell was, as usual, forthright in her opinions.

'You do! Voodoo witch of the woollies!' taunted Johnny, sitting beside her. 'You'd look lovely as a black sheep, me deario.'

'Go black up your bits, bumboy,' Claire retorted. 'No, Luke's got a point. We should mark the occasion. Coloured wavers?'

Phil Leadbetter was annoyed. 'No. Our kit's our brand. Don't go mucking about with it. We want people to think, ah yes, there go the Larksea Morris.'

There were several objections. 'But it's for fun!' 'It's the bonfire society's do, not ours.' 'Everyone knows us anyway.' 'Yes a splash of colour to join in the spirit.'

'I know,' said Claire. 'Red and orange wavers, to look like flames.' The picture caught people's imagination. Hannah asked if there was general agreement.

'Only if it's done properly,' put in Mike. 'We've got to look like a team. Anyone prepared to make a set of matching, decent-sized wavers in orange and red?'

'The bag can cover it,' added Charlie. 'We had a decent haul from those seafront stands.'

'I can get the material cheaply,' volunteered Sarah.

'And I can run them up, no problem,' said Lolly.

'Great. We're in business,' cheered Hannah.

*

Bonfire night was cold, but dry and clear. The procession route was packed with supporters, and the new wavers flashed as high as the torches of the bonfire boys as they capered through the narrow streets. There were some inventive costumes. Two men dressed as medieval knights had jousting horses strapped fore and aft, and they made a pantomime show of charging at each other with crooked lances. The best outfit was a walking, Psycho-style shower curtain that occasionally lit up with a torch from within and let out a scream as tomato ketchup splatted down the side.

At pauses in the procession the side broke off for a dance. 'Funny how we often stop outside a pub, isn't it?' remarked Biff. Alex risked taking the newly rehearsed Mrs Casey out for the first time on the grounds that there probably wouldn't be many morris dancers watching with a critical eye. The slows of the toe-heel-toe looked controlled and smooth, eleven on each side of the set; they made a good single line in the crossovers, but the hand movements were less impressive, lacking co-ordination. Wobbly but promising was Alex's verdict.

As the procession reached the seafront, the public closed in behind, jostling for position. The crush could get scary for kids, but if participants were in kit or costume, they still got to be close to the fire at the end of the parade, and were probably the only ones to hear the Mayor's speech. The town crier clanged his handbell for quiet; his voice carried, the Bonfire President called for three cheers for King James and the Queen which everyone could hear, and all the bonfire society threw their flaming torches onto the brushwood pile. Instantly a great crackle ripped round the bonfire, and a billowing cloud of golden sparks shot up. Drummers really let rip, like a pounding of heartbeats: as if the memory of danger awakened in the crowd.

Suddenly there was a huge explosion in the sky, and all eyes turned to the castle. The drummers were stilled. As the big firework display was at the edge of the cliff, there was no attempt to co-ordinate loud music. The sky filled with chrysanthemums of fire, and the boom of the explosions echoed off the cliff. The massive fire on the beach, the sea surging in the background, the ooh-aahs of the crowd as each spectacular burst of colour filled the sky, all this combined to arouse a feeling of ancient mysteries and rituals. There was a deep collective sigh before the thunderous applause at the end of the show.

The pubs were open late. At The Anchor both bars were heaving with bonfire costumes and sweaty faces, but there was a semi-permanent canvas awning at the back where most of the morris who had children were gathered.

Alex was on a post-performance high, enjoying a whisky chaser with Pete Kershaw. They were discussing how the minor tune of 'Bold Nelson's Praise' could be used as an opener before switching to the major harmonies of 'Princess Royal.' Hannah was also basking in the success of the event, chatting to Lolly.

'I love the timing of Bonfire, don't you? Just when winter begins to bite, whoosh! the fire lights you up inside and you don't mind the evenings closing in.'

'I know what you mean,' said Lolly. 'I found myself dancing on air in the processional, full of the joys. Really takes you out of yourself. Angie was enjoying herself too, wasn't she?' Angie had been allowed to join the procession with coloured wavers, but not in full kit, as she hadn't been voted in yet.

'So was Naomi! I saw her several times weaving in and out alongside the procession with some of her school chums.'

'She loved having her face blackened. It sort of released her inhibitions. But she's no dancer. Her swimming's coming along well though. Could represent the county in her age group.'

'Steve loves swimming too. Did you say Naomi goes to swimming club on a Saturday morning? Could Alex or I bring him? I know he'd like that. Funny boy. Quite self-effacing one minute, then competitive the next.'

'Oh yes. They do exercises and techniques and games as well as races. I'm sure Naomi would be pleased to see someone else she knows.'

'Settled, then. Probably see you next weekend!'

The two women beamed at each other.

A few people were scattered further out beyond the awning in the dark of the pub garden. Hannah noticed Brandon standing on his own. She went over.

'As good a turnout as last year,' she smiled.

'Better, I think. I'm really glad we ditched the torches in favour of those wavers. Sarah's touch of finding material with some gold thread was really effective. And I'm sure your Angie will be voted in before next year.'

'Maybe a bit soon. I've made it slightly awkward by insisting newcomers aren't voted in till the foreman says so. Can't have Alex accused of favouritism.'

Brandon sniffed. 'Minor matter. It always looks good to have a few real youngsters in the set, and Angie is a natural dancer. No-one reasonable is going to think Alex is unfair.'

'Thanks. I'm glad. I must say I haven't noticed much resentment or politicking after the turnabout at the AGM. I really hadn't expected to be squire. You sure you're all right about it? When I saw you alone just now...'

'Yes, fine. It's a relief in many ways. I did enjoy leading when things went well. But it's a heck of a lot of work. You must be finding that, even coming in to the quiet season. Carol's a good secretary, but all those phone calls and making lists and trying to get people to pay attention at the meeting, blimey! They don't talk across you in the way they often did with me.'

Brandon paused. 'Actually, it may be a blessing I didn't go for it. This is in confidence, Hannah, but I'm looking for another job. I don't want to move right out of the area, but I'd like a promotion, well, a change, anyway. I'm not going to get it where I am.'

'Oh, I thought you were happy at Maywood. Not a bad school. Angie likes it. And you know you're a good teacher.'

Her warmth and sincerity touched Brandon. 'Yes, I was just sort of at ease there. But things haven't been going so well lately. Stress of inspection. Some stupid changes. I, erm...' He took a gulp of beer, looking into Hannah's open, friendly face. 'Well, another confidence. Things haven't been going too well at home, either. Zoe's gone a bit distant, I don't know. She keeps saying things are okay, and we're fine in public, but I can't seem to draw her out. She's not talking to me like she did. The AGM took me by surprise. She sort of implied she felt I should withdraw as squire, didn't she? I felt a bit, you know, undermined. But I don't mind you being squire at all, a bit of a relief, as I say.' He sighed. 'I don't quite know where she's coming from any more.'

'Oh. I... I'm sorry. You both seem such a strong couple. I'm sure it'll work out.' Brandon looked so miserable she wanted to hug him, but they both had glasses in their hands. 'Let me get you a pint. We'll have to go soon. I promise not to tell anyone. But if I can help at all...'

Suddenly she was overwhelmed with sympathy for this tall, handsome man, looking like a lost boy who needs his mother. She spontaneously leant up and kissed him. In a clumsy gesture, glass in hand, he gave her a hug.

'Thanks. I'll come in with you. Alex is a lucky man.'

They did not see Zoe dart back into the bar. She had seen the conversation, the earnest light in their faces, Hannah kissing her man, his arm going round her. She was stung.

Winter

Winter

Chapter 7:
Back to Back

The routines of winter settled in. Practice night conversations were about watching TV, everyday concerns, things quietly germinating underneath. Ordinary, hibernating lives.

But no lives are ordinary; each anguish is unique. Zoe nursed her suspicion. Her first reaction on seeing Brandon and Hannah together had been to confront him immediately. She was seething as she went back into the bar, but when Brandon joined her it was all apparently social and no place for a row. While she kept up the facade of normality, underneath fear began to creep in. Might she really be losing him? And doubts: was what she had seen merely a public show of affection, a little of the usual social glue? She was good at that sort of group camaraderie herself.

By the time they got home, her animus had fizzled out, leaving her anxious and uncertain.

'I'm knackered,' said Brandon. 'Going to flake out. Coming?'

'Not just yet. I'll have a cup of tea and unwind.'

She drifted round the newly-fitted modern kitchen then through the old-style dining room (which she sometimes liked, sometimes didn't), and ended up in her nest armchair by the big window, looking out at the night. She wanted to cling to the old certainties. Big, happy-go-lucky Brandon, who loved her, didn't he? Could he really be having an affair? She had been feeling bored and dissatisfied for some time. Brandon was so predictable, not going anywhere despite some job applications. There was a lethargy between them. Perhaps she could retrain as a teacher herself? She'd be better than some of them she was sure. What she didn't want was people to feel she was failing in her relationship.

They had got through difficulties before. Who could she confide in? Someone warm and trustworthy. Lolly. Good-hearted, reliable Lolly.

Her opportunity came at a tune-up a few days later. The back bar at The Anchor was a bit cramped, but with the doors open on to the patio under the awning, the keen ones could crowd round, and the talkers sitting further back didn't disturb the musicians. All seemed pleasant enough. Brandon was with her, and Ray and Lolly had got Amy Kershaw, Pete's wife, to babysit. Amy wasn't a fan of a long evening as a bystander, watching Pete enjoy himself, and she was no singer. Lolly on the other hand always enjoyed a tune-up, even an endless round of Speed the Plough. It wasn't till quite late in the evening that Zoe spotted her moment to ask Lolly to come into the front bar for a drink. There were quite a few people in there, chatting. They wouldn't be overheard.

'I'll have an Archer's please,' said Lolly, 'but I'll have to go back for the massed melodeons at the end.'

'Plenty of time. I'm going to be wicked and have a Baileys. Wasn't Pete's "Adieu Sweet Lovely Nancy" good?'

'Yes, and his penny whistle's been a treat too. Really soars over the rest.' They settled to their drinks.

'Lolly, I've got something tricky to ask you. I don't suppose there's anything in it, but at Bonfire I happened to see Hannah giving Brandon a kiss. I know it's silly of me, but it's got me a bit worried. I wondered if you've noticed anything? Heard anything, perhaps?'

'No, I haven't noticed anything. They seem to get on in an ordinary, friendly way.' She paused, and drew a deep breath. 'But I'm afraid I did hear a rumour that something might be going on. I'd never believe it of Hannah, though, would you? And you certainly can't trust gossip. People just seem to like speculating.'

'Oh. I see. No-one's said anything to me, as you'd expect. Can I ask who you heard it from?'

'This is difficult. Please don't say I told you, but it was Carol. She asked me if I'd heard anything, and of course I said no, and she hasn't referred to it since.'

'How long ago?'

'Several weeks. I'm sure you don't need to set much store by it.' Lolly winced. She hated being involved in emotional tangles like this. 'Why don't you ask Brandon straight out? I can see it'd be difficult, of course.'

'I'm thinking about it. I need some time. I'm certainly not rushing off to Carol. She can be a bitch. I wouldn't give her the pleasure.'

Zoe felt pinched. She dare not confront Brandon. If he admitted it was true, she couldn't bear the feeling of betrayal and failure; if he denied it, her own mistrust meant she couldn't believe him. A thread of anger spilled over from her envy of Alex, too. He's got everything, she thought, serve him right if his wife's unfaithful to him. Let him suffer like the rest of us.

She took Lolly's hand. 'Oh dear. What a tangled web we weave.' She was clearly upset and vulnerable, so Lolly just patted her hand reassuringly, and released it to pick up her drink. They went back in to the tune-up.

Just as they came in, it was Biff's turn. He put his guitar down and called above the chatter, 'You all know the chorus.' A hush fell as he launched into:

'What's the life of a man, any more than a leaf?
A man has his seasons, so why should he grieve?
And though in this world we appear fine and gay,
Like the leaf we must wither, and soon fade away.'

Biff had put his heart into the sadness of the song. Only a flicker passed over people's faces as they sang the old use of the word gay.

As he finished there were calls of 'Good man, Biff,' and muted but sincere applause. Zoe was genuinely moved. In her heightened emotional state, the line 'when age and affliction upon us has called' made her feel how fragile and short-lived everything was.

Ray saw a glitter in her eye, and moved round. 'Sentimental old song, but it gets me every time,' he said in apparent sympathy. 'Seems to belong to a simpler, better world, something we've lost.'

Zoe nodded. 'I know, I know, I love it.' She found a tissue. 'It's like the Copper songs. Lives and stories and suffering. Real romance too. I suppose their songs cast a spell for them, that's how they could escape from the hardship of their times. A lot more than just feel-good. Eternal love, fidelity and all that.' She disguised a sob with a sniff.

Ray was quick to pick up on her mood, drawn to her glistening eyes, the lustre of her black hair. 'You all right, Zoe?'

'Yes yes. Just the song. Silly me.' They stood together, saying no more. Pete began singing the Farewell Shanty.

'Time for us to leave you.
Haul away to heaven...'

Ray slipped his arm round Zoe's waist. In her needy state, Zoe felt a rush of gratitude, and affection. I've met a strong man, she thought.

*

Once a month through the autumn and winter, local bands hosted a ceilidh up at the school sports hall. When funds were up to it, they afforded a band of folk festival quality. Tonight's was a treat: the Foaming Firkins were up from Portsmouth. Their line-up included a hurdy-gurdy and a good alto sax player.

Alex and Hannah took the children. It was a frosty evening. Steve was hopping along, excited by being allowed to come, and thrilled by the night sky. He was fascinated by how much bigger the Great Bear was than just the Plough. Stars flickered and flashed. He pointed out orange Aldebaran, to the right of Orion.

'It's so far away but think if it was our sun!' His voice got higher. 'The whole sky would be red and gold!'

'But would we still have our Goldilocks zone?' Alex asked, walking ahead quickly. 'Life's pretty fragile here on the blue pearl. Is Aldebaran a red giant?'

'Wait, wait!' Steve called. 'I want to see a shooting star.' But the warm lights of the hall beckoned, and they hurried inside.

There was quite a bustle in the hall as the first dance, a Sicilian circle, was called. Cold feet made people clumsy, but there was plenty of goodwill. The second dance was a rant step so they were soon thawed out and into the swing of it. The ceilidh had attracted quite a range of people from beyond the morris, and the caller was clear, not presuming everyone knew the figures. The confident dancers threw themselves into it, carrying the newcomers with them.

Ray had started by dancing with Lolly, but was flattered when a young woman he didn't know asked him to dance. Then he danced with Hannah in a complicated four pairs set. He felt flushed and exhilarated, dancing with such an agile, sure-footed partner.

The morris were mostly sitting together. Hannah and Lolly got up together to join the queue for the bar during a breather. They were pleased how well Steve and Naomi were getting on at swimming club. The caller announced the Rosa waltz. Lolly stayed at the bar, so Ray turned to Zoe. He stood with a mock bow and said, 'Could I have this dance, my lady?' Zoe raised her eyebrows to Brandon but he just smiled. Up she got.

Both knew the steps backwards, so they could let themselves glide. In the arms-around each other sequence, Ray spoke gently in her ear. 'This is nice. Wish life could always be like this.'

Zoe felt expansive, relaxed. The little world of the waltz felt secure, how couples ought to be, balanced, familiar, affectionate. She was very aware of Ray's body, his supple movements and his firm hold.

Then out of the corner of her eye she saw Brandon dancing with Hannah. She instantly stiffened. Ray followed her gaze, but said nothing. Zoe regained her composure, and they waltzed on.

When they sat down, Brandon turned to Zoe. 'You up for the next?'

'I'll just sit for this one,' she said, looking at Hannah with her children, thinking, I wonder, I wonder, surely she wouldn't... Brandon turned to Lolly. 'This one's got a strip- the- willow. Would you like to?'

Lolly was on her feet without hesitation. 'Yes. Great. I love this tune. Really gets your feet twitching.'

They walked to the floor without taking hands, but Lolly could feel a blush rising as she matched Brandon's easy stroll. While they waited, he jogged up and down a few times. She grinned at him and hopped a bit herself. Such infectious, boyish good humour. He was strong enough to lift her off her feet.

Alex and Hannah were in the same set, with Angie doing a good job of helping Steve, who was all over the place, like an enthusiastic puppy. The hurdy-gurdy was in this arrangement. Hannah loved the peculiar drone and skirl, a sound both antique and merry, that made the feet drive on, a pulsing beat. She and Alex were in a swirl of happiness, the family together, Steve's grin so wide, Brandon and Lolly so energetic and graceful, the whole set turning with a centrifugal force, fire to the fingers, fire to the toes, we're the world, the world's a dance! Hannah wanted to lose herself in it forever.

During the last polka Lolly sat out, breathing deeply, the pleasure of the dance slowly receding. Ray was spinning round with Zoe. She was content to recover, free to think for herself. Naomi was having a sleepover at Tamsin's. She watched Brandon chatting with Alex and Charlie. She sighed. The glow of the dance quickly left her as she thought of the drive home with Ray in a cold car. She wished she could be pleased they were having a night out together. Her mind ran on with thoughts about him. He always did the washing up, that bloke's concession to housework; not much else. His flirting was making her edgy, but she shrank from talking to him about it, afraid of his easy, even sneering dismissal.

With a lurch she realised she really didn't want him to make love to her tonight.

Chapter 8:
Strike Butts

The sea was grey and sluggish, the promenade deserted. On a cold evening early in December, half a dozen of the side settled into a snug corner of The Anchor to discuss the mummers' play. They felt they could allow themselves a bit of a pre-Christmas glow now December had finally come; after all, said Martin, the anticipation was half the pleasure.

Phil Clothier, Mike and Charlie were the main movers, with Biff, Martin and Ray along for the ride. (No Brandon this year; too busy, he'd said.)

'We had a good old roister last year.' Charlie was feeling expansive on rum. 'You made a brilliant Roy the rutting Rover, Biff. And the way you squirted people with that bottle – it really did look like pee.'

'I wouldn't mind playing him again,' chuckled Biff. 'Took me hours to make that bleedin' doggy outfit. Funny how people like the old chestnuts, isn't it? What do you think of it so far?'

'Rough!' Martin woofed obligingly. 'I'm missing that bark already. And you were rather daring, I thought, with the sniffing. But we can't really have Rover again this year, Biff, not with his kidnap 'n' all.'

'How about a send-up of that bloody-minded detective inspector who was such a pain at Bonfire?' asked Ray. 'There's as many old policeman plod jokes as there are doggy ones.'

'Not a bad idea,' said Mike, well into his third pint, 'but I wondered about replacing St George and the Turkish Knight with Punch St George and Judy Nightly. You could work a whole puppet show into the mummers' scenes.'

Martin nodded. 'I like it. Lot of work, though. You'd need to write a good new script. Here's my pennyworth. I think we should do the whole thing in drag. Nothing like a bout of balloon popping to get people going.'

'Ha! Oo-er missus,' said Phil. 'You'd be good at it, but it's not for me. And wouldn't it be confusing if we were all dragged up? Complicated costumes, too.'

After more of this and a few guffaws, they couldn't make up their tipsy minds, and they drifted into the compromise of sticking to the basic text, but each character could bring his own surprise element, jokes, costumes, props, whatever appealed.

'Bloody democracy!' grinned Biff. 'What we need is leadership. Hannah as dominatrix. I'll invite Hitler and Himmler to next year's planning meeting.'

The idea of going in drag appealed to Ray. He thought he could transform his role as Turkish Knight into a bearded lady, maybe try to look like someone- Anne Widdicombe? - no, better still, someone they all knew; yes, of course, send up Hannah as squire. She usually wore distinctive smock tops to practice. A charity shop would be bound to have something similar. And a joke shop blonde wig... He could see it all in his mind's eye, and anticipated the laughs he'd get for his contribution.

They toured the play round four pubs on the Saturday evening before Christmas. Charlie had put up posters, and the landlords were cheerful about it, but the pubs were packed anyway. Several of the side came along for the whole tour, and some partners. Carol Murfin's husband Colin, an inveterate mocker of the morris, said the only justification for any of it was an excuse for a pub crawl. By the time they wound up at The Anchor quite a few more turned up.

Alex was already relaxing at the bar. He'd been with Angie and Steve most of the day while Hannah shopped, and she said he'd earned an hour off. Also, she was watching one of those hospital dramas, not his favourite. He was chatting to Lolly, who hadn't wanted to spend her whole evening traipsing round after the mummers- it seemed a bit blokeish to her. She was happy to find Alex there.

'How's all the preparations going, then?' he asked.

'Easier than yours, I bet. We're going to my parents this year, so it's less hassle. Your family all coming?'

'Just for Christmas Day. But Hannah's folk are staying. Her mum's all right, 'cept when she tries to be jolly with the mother-in-law jokes against herself. Last year in the pub she asked me to get her a mother-in-law's tongue. When I looked blank, she said it was stout and bitter.' He grimaced. 'But she does really get alongside the kids, and helps. Her old man's a go-with-the-flow type, too. Easy to please.'

Not feeling very Christmassy, Lolly wanted to change the subject.

'I've been having a go with an English concertina recently. I love that simpler sound. More breathy, like a human voice. Have you ever tried one?'

'Yes, but it's too much of a change of technique for me. I know what you mean about the tone of it, though. Great to accompany a voice. Doesn't carry so well for dancing out.'

'Oh, I think it could. Just needs a good clear beat underneath. Buy Steve a tabor for Christmas!' Lolly nodded her head, remembering. 'D'you know, the most effective music I've ever heard to accompany the dance was a fife and tabor. It really carries, so uncluttered. Feels old, too. Atmospheric.'

'Mmm... Sort of medieval. But it's got to be really well done. I've heard Pete just use the whistle a couple of times and that worked. You should bring your concertina to practice. See how it goes.'

'I'm not good enough yet, but thanks. Maybe I'll concentrate on working up just a couple of tunes.'

Lolly felt comfortable. It was always positive talking to Alex. He in turn admired her musicianship, and the way she dealt with things with such equanimity. He guessed it couldn't be easy at times. But before they could bask in each other's company any longer, the mummers made their noisy entrance.

By now the performers were confident, with more than a drop taken. Charlie was greeted by a barrage of cheerful jeers as he got up to start.

'In come I, old Father Christmas,
welcome be or welcome not.
I hope old Father Christmas
shall never be forgot.'

Charlie hadn't made much concession to producing new quirky characteristics. He had a bran tub with presents attached by string to the base, so his offerings never escaped, ho ho ho, but he kept the voluminous beard and heavily tasselled red hat he used for swatting people. His Father Christmas with a penchant for domestic violence had become traditional.

Martin was wearing a Prince Charles mask as St George, and acknowledged the catcalls of 'Bog off, Bigears!' with exaggerated low bows. Ray kept a cloak over his outfit before his entrance, and didn't pull his wig on till the last minute. He enjoyed the whistles when he flounced on.

'If you've got 'em, pop 'em!' called Johnny Rendell.
'Turk for squire!' shouted Claire, recognising the smock top.
'In come I, a Turkish Knight,
out of the harem to give you a fright....'

Ray wasn't fazed by all the crude interruptions. He rather overdid his death, even by mumming standards, reviving and expiring four times before the Doctor entered, and the laughter became rather forced. Phil as Doctor had invested in some very large bananas, cucumbers and carrots, offering the Turkish Lady and the audience some very suggestive choices.

Ray squeaked:
'Oh Doctor Brandon, Doctor Brandon, heal me, squeeze me, push me parsley...'

The Doctor performed a rather obvious operation, and the Lady puckered up for a clumsy kiss before his balloons were popped by an enormous carrot.

There was desultory applause and one or two knowing glances amongst the audience. Alex picked up the undercurrent and joined in the laughter half-heartedly. Lolly's serious expression gave him a twinge of unease. The play swept on with Mike as a Chief Constable arresting at random and handcuffing nearly willing victims to the tables, with the usual ribald remarks about truncheons and policemen's helmets.

Afterwards, Ray came up to Lolly and Alex expecting admiration, too full of himself to notice a lukewarm reception.

'Good old mummers. Old jokes, new references. Always works a treat. I think the bag should subsidise my balloons. Well, enjoyable or what?'

'Lovely, dear.' Lolly's irony was both friendly and sarcastic. Alex grinned, guessing what she really thought. Ray couldn't resist a direct question.

'What did you think, Alex?'

'Couldn't have done it in worse taste myself,' joshed Alex, looking at Lolly.

Johnny loomed tipsily between them.

'Aha, the naughty nigel himself, the knight with the 'normous breastplates. Well done, you vast plum pillock.'

He drew Ray over to Biff and Charlie who were revelling in the Christmas bonhomie, arguing about whether it would add to the play if they invited a rapper side from Brighton over to take part next year, or whether it would steal the show.

Alex was happy to leave them to it. Feeling thoughtful, he turned to Lolly.

'Was I meant to be rattled by Ray's Doctor Brandon stuff?' he asked quietly. 'Just part of the usual banter? It felt a bit barbed.'

'Well, you know Ray. I'm afraid he does enjoy winding people up. And... oh dear. Yes. There have been a few mutterings, Alex. I mean about how well Hannah and Brandon get on. Silly stuff, you know, don't take it seriously.'

'Really? Hmm... I've got to ask. Who's been saying things?'

'Just the gossipmongers, you know, Carol, Amy too.' Lolly felt very awkward. 'This was weeks ago. I'm sure you can ignore it.'

'I wonder if Hannah knows but hasn't wanted to say anything. Probably a way of getting at her because she's squire? I'd like to find out a bit more.'

'You're not upset, are you?'

'No, but it's good to know what's going on. I'm surprised no-one's mentioned it before. Heigh ho. Another drink?'

And they left it there. Despite his denial, Alex was troubled, not by any real doubts about Hannah, but how it could have come about. Damn people's sneakiness. Particularly Ray. He wanted more information before he said anything to Hannah, and managed not to let it bother him over thc Sunday after the mummers' play.

At the Monday practice, he cornered Carol straight away.

'Carol, I've got a bone to pick with you.' She looked alarmed. Alex didn't usually look so intense and serious. 'Have you been spreading rumours about Hannah having an affair with Brandon?'

Carol eyes shifted. 'Not really spreading rumours, no. I heard something and asked a couple of people what they thought. That's all.'

'Who did you hear it from'? Alex was glaring.

'Ray, actually. It was weeks ago. Sorry. Only repeating what I heard.'

'Well, don't repeat it,' snapped Alex, and stalked away.

Once they got home and the children were in bed, he waited till they had cleared the kitchen and made some tea before he spoke to Hannah.

'I've picked up a rumour, love, side gossip, but I can't ignore this one – it's personal.' He tugged at his sideburns. 'Um, a couple of people are saying that you may be having a fling with Brandon.'

'Good God, no. Of course not. Why on earth...' Hannah put her teacup down slowly. 'Alex, you duffer, you haven't taken it seriously, have you?'

'No, I haven't, not for a moment.' There was nevertheless a small knot dissolved for him, a reassurance, and a rush of warmth towards Hannah. 'Have any of the women hinted or said anything to you?'

'Not a dickeybird. For heaven's sake, Alex, you know I'd have told you anyway.'

'I know, I know. Just as I've told you. Don't be angry.'

'Well, not at you. But it's spiteful of people to say things like that. Is it because I'm squire? I thought things were going quite well.'

'Yes, I wondered about that. And you are doing well. But here's the thing...' and he told her about Ray's get-up at the mummers and the Doctor Brandon lines, and Lolly's gentle confession about how she'd heard something from Carol, leading back to Ray.

'Nasty how a lie can travel,' Hannah remarked tartly. 'I mean, Brandon's a good-looking man, half the women on the side fancy him, but they've always joked openly about it, like you and I joke about it when we fancy someone.' She flicked her eyebrows at him. 'No, it's Ray we need to sort out, nasty weasel. He needs to know what we think.'

Alex breathed in. 'So what do you think I should do? I did tell Carol off tonight, but Ray... I could confront him, of course, but I don't suppose it'd do any good. No doubt he'd pretend it was just a Chinese whisper, some casual thing he'd said that's got blown out of proportion.'

'At least he'd know we were on to him. But hold on...' She wrinkled her nose. 'Two can play at that game. I could fancy winding him up in turn – not make nasty rumours about him – perhaps say some things to him straight out, no problem – um...' She turned her mug of tea round thoughtfully. 'I know.

How about if I pretend to flirt with him, make him think I fancy him? I'd have to let a few people know what I was doing. We could both speak to Lolly, make sure she's ok with it, reassure her I'm not after her fella, explain why I'm doing it. I don't think she'll mind- she's said before she's used to his flirting.'

'OK,' said Alex, not wholly convinced.

'And I'll speak to Carol, say I've no ill will or anything about the Brandon rumour, and let her in our little game.' Hannah warmed to her theme. 'I don't mind Carol. Shoots her mouth off a bit, but there's no malice in her. She'd enjoy it. Probably tell others, get them in on the joke. Oh dear, am I doing a Ray myself?'

'No, not really, he deserves it, but don't let it go on too long before you tell him straight what you really feel.' He leant back on the sofa. 'Besides, I might get jealous.'

'Oh yeah? We'll have to do something about that.' She got up and straddled herself on his lap.

They kissed, and went upstairs.

Chapter 9:
Half Hey

At their Christmas dinner table, Hannah's mother was looking flushed. A couple of extra visits to the bottle of Bailey's had eased her through the tensions of the final assembly – last year she had dropped the hot tray of roast potatoes on the kitchen floor – and now she was relaxed and smiling broadly. She didn't have much in common with Alex's parents, but as she said to Hannah, she liked them well enough to play happy families.

Alex made a ceremony of untwisting the wire on the sparkling wine. It went off like a gunshot. Angie shrieked in excitement and alarm. Only a few bubbles escaped.

'A toast, everyone.' He beamed round the table. The usual collection of ill-fitting paper hats beamed back. 'We've passed the longest night. Happy Christmas!' Calls of Happy Christmas came back warmly as glasses chinked.

Zoe's parents and elder sister Cynthia had arrived on Christmas Eve. They got through the first meal quite politely with a pretence at pleasure, but Cynthia had to sleep on the sofabed and made it quite clear what she thought of it. Zoe was on tenterhooks, but managed to hold her tongue, saying to herself that she'd give Cynthia a choice piece of her mind if she made any catty remarks about the food. She darted round the kitchen, trying not to be irritated by her mother's helpful suggestions. Cynthia had been regaling them with her new job and was very full of it, dropping names of wealthy clients and the restaurants she'd been to on her expense account. Zoe's father pretended to be chivalrous, but was really quite pompous and selfish. What a wind-up, sighed Zoe, and gritted her teeth; the whole thing was about as welcome as an overcooked brussel sprout.

Now driving with Brandon to the Boxing Day lunchtime stand at The Anchor, Zoe's frustrations were seething. Brandon was withdrawn. He'd had no luck with his job applications, and he was in the doldrums. He hadn't managed to put much spark into jollying the family party along, and sat slumped as Zoe drove impatiently, his big frame jolting at each squeal of brakes.

Zoe was rattling through her irritations, and turned on him.

'Fat lot of use you were last night, agreeing to let Cynthia choose Scrabble. You know she's good at it.'

'Just leave it, Zoe. It was only a game.'

'A game to get at me.' She felt waspish. 'And I've got a bone to pick with you. People have been talking about goings on between you and Hannah Mrs sweetness-and-light Tavener. I saw you kiss her at Bonfire.'

Seconds of silence while Brandon absorbed this slap.

Then he said quietly: '*She* kissed me at Bonfire, Zoe. I was feeling low and she's, well, kind. That's all.'

He overcame a strong desire to lash out and add, unlike you.

'Well what am I meant to think?' snapped Zoe.

'You can think what you bloody well like. These "rumours" are just rubbish. Why have you been sitting on poisonous crap like this for so long?'

Zoe was manoeuvring to park. This was no time to voice her dismay. Her stomach was churning too much to find any words of apology. Both slammed their doors and they stomped into the pub in silence.

At least the bar was neutral ground. If anyone did notice that they both looked like thunder, the moment was quickly covered by the habitual greetings and convivial atmosphere in the crowded room.

The regulars were out in force, including Margo (loudest voice in Larksea), Bert (wandering hands) and Tom (a bore with a Father Christmas hat), all trying to get their fingers on the free nibbles by the pump handles. Landlord Ted was bustling with seasonal bonhomie.

Most of the morris were already belled up, and the jangle added to the air of a survivors' party, with overloud guffaws about what had happened on Christmas Day, and a general expansiveness. Alex called for everyone to form up for a massed Mrs Casey in the narrow street in front of the pub.

It had come on to rain. There was hardly a soul about, but none of the dancers hesitated about going outside. There were a few grumbles, but Charlie berated them cheerfully.

'Load of softies! When did a bit of weather bother us? You always dance on Boxing Day. Three cheers for Cecil Sharp!'

There were two-and-a half jeery cheers.The great man might not have been too pleased with this particular performance. The ritual, ceremonial dance he venerated was full of good-humoured chatter, the toe-heel-toe was totally unco-ordinated, and the hands across the set degenerated into several mock scuffles. Alex was laughing so much he shouted, 'Shambles! Disaster! Abandon ship!'

Everyone piled back into the pub and good sense prevailed – they would continue the dancing under the canvas awning at the back, and anyone could choose a dance if they could get a set up. Zoe danced nearly everything; Brandon stayed at the bar, and found himself intrigued by a conversation between Luke and Biff, who were trying to invent a Wii morris game.

'Two players, each in charge of one side of the set,' said Luke.

'How about three players, each having one of the couples?' Biff suggested.

'No, too complicated. You want straight competition, you know, things like plus points for co-ordination and penalties for mistakes.'

'How about deliberate sabotage? Points for a cunning success, penalties if you got rumbled. You could have a lot of laughs bumping in to people.'

'Yes! Contrive a stick accident. You could take it out on people. I could make suggestions about who to hit.' Luke nodded in Zoe's direction. 'Look at her now, nose in the air, not a smile anywhere. Zap! Extra points for a really good disruption.'

'Ha! You'd deserve penalties for causing it.' Biff had become aware of

Brandon listening in, and included him. 'You could have levels of difficulty, couldn't you? Starter level something like Come Landlord, next hocklebacks and leapfrogs, right up to Shepherds Hey Fieldtown. Nobody gets the pause on the flourish right, and the dance isn't called. No safety net. What do you think, Brandon?'

'I like it. Plusses for height and good lines, penalties for losing a waver. Big bonus for tripping someone up.' Brandon's suggestions got more inventive and aggressive. Biff's became quite obscene.

'Talking of knob-knocking, you coming to the New Year's Day Border this year?' Biff asked.

'No,' said Brandon. 'I intend to get hog-snarling pissed on New Year's Eve and just sleep it off at home.'

'Shame. It's always a laugh. And hair of the dog and all that.'

'Well, we'll see,' said Brandon.

*

A few of the side had set up the New Year's Day Border stand some years previously. The preparatory workshops in December were open to anyone, and they attracted a mix of dancers from the whole town, including kids, who loved to black up and wear rag coats. It wasn't intended to be a very skilled display, but it was a good chance to dance around the town knocking at the doors of friends and acquaintances, who often provided hot drinks. There were enough experienced dancers to hold it together.

Hangovers and hangers-on gathered in the town centre around eleven. It was a bright day, with that particular brightness that proximity to the sea brings, but not a day to linger on the seafront; the wind was icy. There were a surprising number of people about, blowing away the cobwebs, and bystanders had those 'What on earth are they doing now?' grins on their faces as the little procession took off, pushchairs piled with coats and rucksacks trailing behind.

Naomi had decided to tag along this year. She was encouraged to see several people she knew from school obviously enjoying themselves. Outside Phil and Amy Kershaw's house a knot of well-wishers had gathered, and some were enthusiastically persuaded to join in. Safety in numbers, Naomi felt, and lined up opposite a boy from her class who was usually quite shy. Lolly was pleased to see her letting go and even whooping a bit, a good colour in her cheeks. Ray was being boisterous, exaggerating the sticking with wild clashes and barging around in the reels. He joined in vigorously with singing:

'Oh there ain't no hairs on my cat's tail,
there ain't no hairs on Tiny,
but I know where there's lots of hairs
on the girl I left behind me.'

He took off to find himself partnered by Hannah. She had positioned herself carefully to be in a dance with an arms-around figure to start her teasing campaign, and made sure she gave him a good squeeze. Putting on her broadest smile, she panted, 'You're on good form!' and Ray responded with a knowing grin.

At the end of the dance she looked straight at him, and said, 'You're so together, Ray,' then winked, and steeled herself to pinch his bum.

Surprised, he chuckled, and said, 'Mmm... Not so bad yourself.'

The procession moved off, leaving Hannah to find her children. A wave of self-reproach swept over her. 'What am I doing?' she thought. 'Here I am plotting and being deceitful, playing games like silly kids in the playground. I joined the morris for the love of the dance, the coming together, the harmony of it all, the music.' She blinked back a sudden image of the castle green, the dancers circling in the early May sunshine. 'I'm no better than the gossipers,' she sighed.

With relief, she caught up with Angie and Steve.
'It's good, this, isn't it!' said Steve, skipping along.
'Yes darling, it really is,' said Hannah, giving him a hug.

Zoe bounded up to Lolly, her breath coming out in white puffs like a dragon. 'Ray's enjoying himself, isn't he? And flirting with Hannah.'

'Oh, he often flirts.' Lolly refused to be drawn.

'But with Hannah? She was really buttering him up. Bit sly, that.'

'Oh, no, don't be silly. Hannah's not like that at all.'

'I wouldn't be so sure if I were you. It's your bloke she's leading on.'

'You're quite wrong.' Lolly was roused now. 'I know Hannah. I don't know why you're being bitchy.'

'Bitchy? Huh. You're just too kind and loyal to see it. Open your eyes, Lolly. People aren't nearly as nice as you'd like to think.'

'Stop it, Zoe. Your problem is you just want to see the worst in people.'

'Huh!' Zoe sneered. 'Enjoy your comfy little world.'

Lolly turned away. She said nothing.

Hannah found Lolly at the back of the procession.

'I've done it. I've set him up,' she said.

'I know,' said Lolly, looking pinched. 'Zoe's just been warning me about you and your wicked ways.'

'Really? Oh dear. I suppose that's what happens if you play this sort of charade. I feel a bit sort of dirty and devious.'

Lolly shook her head. 'No need to, really. It's just a bit of a lark.' She patted Hannah's arm. 'It's not going to hurt Ray much, anyway. Water off a duck's back.'

'Call it off any time if you want to,' said Hannah. 'Look, Alex has got some winter warmer in his flask. Want a sip?' She pulled Lolly over to where Alex was explaining about the Border tradition to some interested bystanders.

As soon as he saw Lolly he said, 'Good for Naomi! Didn't she do well. She'll be a dancer yet.'

Hannah reached for the hipflask in his pocket and offered it.

Lolly smiled wanly and sipped the whisky.

Chapter 10:
Face to Face

'Hello Hannah, you minx.' Ray's eyebrows twitched as he gave her what he thought was a saucy grin. It was the first practice night after New Year.

'Evening, Ray. Sorry – got to sort out a bit of admin with Carol.' Hannah walked quickly over to where Carol was chatting to Amy at the kitchen hatch at the side of the scout hall. The last thing she wanted was to start the evening pretending to flirt with Ray.

'We had such a good party after the dancing on New Year's Day,' Amy was saying to Carol. 'The Border put us all in the mood, and lunchtime drinking's the best, isn't it? Everyone was getting on so we...' She smiled broadly at Hannah.

Oh Lord, thought Hannah. Is she hinting that she spotted me and Ray? The sooner this stops, the better. She and Alex had only dropped in at Amy's for a quick drink once the dancing had finished, as Angie and Steve were meeting up with their own friends in the afternoon. To Hannah's relief there had been no time for a repeat of the flirting, and Ray had been quite drunk and occupied with a singaround. Tonight was Ray's first opportunity.

Hannah went over to where Lolly was sitting in her usual corner. 'If I don't get a chance to speak later,' she said quietly, 'I'm going to tell Ray tonight. Get the charade over with. I can't bear it! I don't know what I was thinking of.'

'Really, don't worry,' said Lolly. 'As I said, I don't think it'll bother him, make him grumpy or anything like that. But thanks for letting me know – and good luck!' The two women exchanged a friendly glance.

Practice was as noisy as usual. Alex wanted as many people as possible to have a go at calling a dance. Lolly decided to risk it. She enjoyed practice nights, getting absorbed in the music, and the sheer physical exertion took her out of herself. Otherwise she found herself dwelling on a sinking feeling that life with Ray had become dutiful and unrewarding. She volunteered to call 'The

Valentine,' and was focussing on getting her wavers just right and not turning too far in the sidesteps when suddenly the next call was upon her. She had a moment of blind panic.

'Next figure!' she yelled.

The side moved like clockwork into the back-to-back chorus. 'Pick a call, any call!' shouted Martin, with grins all round – and much joking afterwards. Lolly had a strong sense of friends rallying round, and was buoyed up by the confident team spirit. Good old morris, she thought, always there in support when you're feeling down. Alex said she'd started a tradition.

Hannah hadn't been able to divert herself very easily during the evening, and singled out Ray as soon as she could after the meeting.

'Ray, a word.' His unctuous smirk made her heart sink. She kept her voice quiet and controlled, deciding on the direct approach. 'I'm sorry, but, well... I was winding you up on New Year's Day. I'm sorry, but, well – don't fancy you at all. I found out you'd started a rumour about me and Brandon having an affair.'

Ray's face froze.

'It made me angry and I wanted to get back at you. It was stupid of me. Sorry. But don't start any more false stories. For the good of the side.'

Ray was expressionless for a moment, then he shrugged. 'I just thought...'

Hannah cut him off. 'No, you didn't. No more of it, please.'

She walked quickly away before he could say more.

Two nights later, Ray had arranged for Zoe to babysit while he and Lolly went to the cinema. When he fetched her, he decided to tell her about Hannah.

'She had a go at me after practice, really picky. Accused me of being a rumour-monger. You remember she was all flirty at Border? Well she told me she was just trying to get back at me.'

Zoe gave him a sideways glance. 'Really? Thought she was giving you a dose of your own medicine? Bit odd. Maybe she was flirting and then got embarrassed.'

'Doubt it. I don't mind. No skin off my nose. But it's not like her, is it?'

'Well, I s'pose not. Sure you're not annoyed? I'd be furious.'

'No, it's funny really. I just wanted you to know...' He was careful not to mention why Hannah was annoyed with him. Zoe was suddenly preoccupied.

Lolly's defence of Hannah flashed into her mind. Perhaps I have been a bit bitchy, she thought. I'll make my peace with Lolly. Apologise for what I said about Hannah.

*

January wore on, grey and flat. During practice one night, several of the side, including Brandon and Lolly, were entertaining themselves by suggesting ways to bring some contemporary dance into the traditional movements.

'Put in a break dancing figure,' said Sarah, young enough to have the flexibility.

'Or go all Californian, like the side in "*Morris: A Life with Bells On.*"' Luke was equally enthusiastic.

'Too athletic!' exclaimed Claire. 'Mind you, anything to stop becoming as bland as line dancing.'

Alex was starting the next dance, but Brandon and Lolly continued.

'I don't really see it,' said Brandon. 'You've got to be careful. Things like bopping around would just look silly. Something new needs to blend in properly.'

'You could work a bit of rock'n'roll in,' suggested Lolly. 'I don't mind innovation at all. Look at Redbournestoke.'

'Yes, they're good, but they don't do things like putting a bit of the twist into a figure. Twizzles, fine, but it's got to develop from the morris style.'

Alex had come over to ask them to join in the next dance. 'What are you two cooking up now?' he asked.

'Nothing, Mr Foreman, sir,' Brandon said in a schoolboy voice.

'Oh yes you are,' Alex retorted. He raised an eyebrow at Lolly. 'Is this young man molesting you, Miss Haywood?'

Lolly smiled at him, and looked at Brandon.

'No, not yet,' she replied, surprised by her own cheekiness.

At the end of practice they found themselves lingering as others left, almost at a loose end. Ray had stayed at home to babysit for once, and Brandon had given Zoe's excuses. She 'wasn't feeling too bright,' and people had expressed concern. It was very unusual for her to miss practice.

'Can I walk back with you, Lolly? I fancy the air,' Brandon asked.

'Yes, sure. I'd be glad of the company.'

The relaxation of the evening carried them on. The cold was invigorating in the empty streets. Lolly felt emboldened to tell Brandon about the 'bit of fun' Hannah had had at Ray's expense.

'You didn't mind?' asked Brandon. 'I mean it's not like her really, and it could have gone a bit sour.'

'No, it's ok, it was just a little getting back at him for being a rumourmonger.' She hesitated. 'Brandon, you knew he'd said something about you and Hannah having a fling, don't you?'

'Oh, it was *him,* was it? Zoe didn't mention that. We had a bit of a row about it, actually. Her lack of trust got to me a bit. I mean, I've always enjoyed flirting, but I don't mean anything by it. It's just a way of saying you like someone, really.' He flicked his scarf over his shoulder and turned to look at her. 'And I like someone flirting back. I need that kind of pat on the back. I don't function well with people I feel are always going to be critical. Not good at confrontation.'

'I know what you mean. I've got used to Ray's sarcasm. It used not to bother me. But I'm afraid it's got to me recently.'

'I wondered if you were a bit depressed. It's the same with me, actually. I can't seem to do anything right. Zoe's constantly irritated with me. Or worse, just cold. I've been sleeping on the sofa since Christmas. It's knocked me right down.' He paused, uncertain whether to go on. 'I keep up a facade in public. Well, you have to, don't you?'

'You do brilliantly. You always try to be positive. I'm so sorry you're in a bad patch.' She wanted to hug him. There was a pause.

'Lolly, there's something I wanted to ask you...'

He could not see her face. Lolly's heart was in her mouth.

'I've wondered if there was a special feeling between you and Zoe. You get on well, I know, babysitting and all, and she's very warm towards you...'

The shock of disappointment made Lolly sharper than she would otherwise have been. She thought he was going to ask what she felt about him, not Zoe.

'Special? No. She can be very touchy-feely, very nice. She's been quite a prop these last few months. But I do wonder. If anything, I suspect she has a special feeling for Ray.'

'Mmm... Must say I've had similar thoughts, but I'm in no position to accuse people of flirting. It's just that sometimes...'

'I know, I know. But there are people I feel I can trust, I mean really like, wholeheartedly. Like you, Brandon. Not Zoe.'

Brandon swallowed.

'Thanks. Thank you. Lolly, I...' He could scarcely voice the words. He stopped and began to turn to her. She reached out and buried her face in his shoulder.

They held each other for what felt like a long time. His coat felt soft and warm, and he nuzzled her hair. Then he pulled away awkwardly, and took her hand. They walked on. Nearing her house, Lolly disengaged. Neither knew what to say, or what to think beyond the shared moment.

'Will you come in for a cuppa?' Lolly asked.

'Thanks, but no. I ought to be getting back. Thanks, I...'

Lolly looked at him, and from somewhere deep inside a smile slowly radiated. She nodded.

'Good night, then. See you soon.'

'Yes,' he said, finding a wry smile in return, and with a self-conscious wave, he walked away.

*

Next morning, after Ray had left for work, Lolly and Naomi were chatting over their bowls of cocopops, when out of the blue Naomi said:

'Zoe popped in last night. I was in bed so I didn't get up to say hello. I thought she might've been coming to babysit, you know, so Dad could go down the pub, but she just stayed for a bit.'

'Oh. Mmm... She may have had some business with Dad about school property or something. Finish up, darling, or we'll be late.'

Lolly covered the internal roar of her suspicion with breakfast bustle.

*

The night had taken Ray by surprise, too.

Zoe had phoned, obviously in a bit of a state, saying she needed to talk. 'A bit of therapy, please,' she said. Ray suggested she could come round for half an hour, and she jumped at it. 'Just push the door open,' he said.

'This is kind,' she said as he greeted her in the hallway. They made a coffee and settled on the sofa. Zoe pitched straight in.

'You can guess what this is about. It must be obvious Brandon and I haven't been getting on for some time. I don't think he's having an affair or anything, but he just hasn't been there for me for ages.'

'I'm so sorry,' said Ray. 'You put up a pretty good front, I must say.'

'The atmosphere at home is awful. He mopes around the flat, doesn't want to do anything, and sometimes he looks at me as if... as if... Oh God, I think he hates me.' Her eyes were very bright.

'You poor old thing,' said Ray. He moved closer and put his arm round her shoulder, very conscious of her spicy perfume and the silky feel of her blouse.

Zoe sighed heavily, ending in a little sob. She rested her head on Ray's arm, and let a tear run down her cheek. She was very aware of the need to be quiet with Naomi in the house.

She detached herself from him and reached into her bag for a tissue.

'Oh dear. Sorry about that.' She sniffed as she leant forward to pick up her coffee. Ray watched her skirt ride up past her knees.

'Not at all, not at all. I'm just so sorry to see you like this. What's brought it all on, really?'

Zoe poured out her doubts, all the little things that seemed to have gone wrong, the way she couldn't find her old feeling for Brandon. He was so moody, he hated school, he wasn't getting anywhere with job applications – and he was sleeping on the sofa.

Ray listened, nodding and murmuring sympathy, all the time feeling a tidal pull as he looked at her beautiful pale skin, her rich black hair tied loosely with a turquoise scarf, the swell of her breasts.

'Brandon's got no idea how lucky he is,' he said, breathing fast.

He put his hand on her thigh.

Zoe went quiet. She looked at him directly, her heart thudding, and felt a shutter come down on her thoughts. It was a kind of mental shrug: damn the consequences. She let herself be drawn by the tingle of that touch, that sympathy, acceptance, admiration: warmth at last.

He kissed her.

After a few moments, Zoe sat back, straightening her skirt. She drew a deep breath. 'I mustn't stay any longer.'

'No, but we must meet soon. I'll text you at school.'

'Yes. Good.'

At the door, Ray helped her into her coat, and gave her a formal peck on the cheek. She squeezed his hand.

'Take care now, won't you, hm?' he said as he opened the door quietly, and watched her disappear into the January night.

Chapter 11:
First Corners

Zoe always kept a leaf from the previous year's Jack in the Green in her purse as a talisman. She would often touch it for good luck, to summon strength, and silently visualise the Jack in spring sunshine radiating energy.

The day after her conversation with Ray, she dressed warmly after work and walked up to the castle green. There was still some light at five o'clock, but the sea was wintry with white horses and the wind stung her face. No one about. She took the leaf from her bag, collected herself and placed it solemnly on the grass. Taking a few deep breaths, she walked around it three times, thinking of the Jack dancing, and murmured to herself:

Come, Old One, come
My heart is your drum
Come, Jack, come.

Then she knelt and kissed the ground, laying her hand on the leaf, and closed her eyes. She conjured up a vision of herself with Ray, hand in hand, walking in the sun, and let the picture slowly fill her mind.

She poured her energy into the vision until it was fixed and fulfilled, then stood, and chanted three times:

By loam and by leaflight
Let this seed grow.

Picking up the leaf, she walked away in the twilight, and thought she felt a gentle glow inside.

The next morning Zoe was at her computer in the headmaster's office when her mobile buzzed. She jumped, then tried to cover her nerves as there was a pupil waiting in the office. As soon as the boy had gone in to see the head, she quickly opened the bottom drawer of her desk where she kept her bag. Yes, a text, from Ray: 'When can we talk?' and ending with a kiss. She texted back: 'Coffee break at 11.10. I'll phone you.' She added two kisses, and realised she was blushing. This is ridiculous, she thought.

At breaktime she went outside promptly. There were a few children playing in the corner of the sports field, but she was confident she wouldn't be overheard. She glanced about, took the mobile from her bag,and tapped the memory key.

'Ray. Thanks for the text.'

'Glad you could get back so quickly. I know you haven't got long. Look, there's a house a couple of miles out of town I'm selling. Owners away this week. Could you meet me there?'

'Erm, I... yes. Thursday's probably best. About half past four? Brandon's got a school play rehearsal. Won't be home till about 6.30.'

'Great. It's a big detached house with grounds...' and he rattled off the address. 'Thursday 4.30. then. Text me if there's anything urgent before that.'

'Right. See you... then.' Ray's phone went silent. Zoe realised she was breathless. Bad as a schoolgirl, she thought, but rather liked the idea. Her mind raced. Thank you, Jack, she whispered. Thursday seemed a week away.

Business was slack at The Body Shop. Lolly checked stock, re-arranged and tidied, but kept thinking of home. Ray wasn't doing anything out of the ordinary, but he was being considerate, fetching Naomi from school, putting up a shelf she'd asked for months ago. She felt miserable to be suspicious, and longed to talk to Hannah. But there was nothing to say, really. Keep going, she said to herself, put one foot in front of the other...

During the week, Brandon found himself in town, pretending that he wasn't aware that he was near The Body Shop, but at the same time conscious that there was still half an hour to closing time. He stopped to look in an old-fashioned ironmongers. What *am* I doing, he thought. I don't want anything here. But he lingered, unable to make himself walk the three doors down to The Body Shop, hoping Lolly might come out. A spontaneous meeting. He longed to talk to her. But what could he say? I can't do this, he thought, and walked back the way he had come. The street had never seemed so long and dreary.

The exhilaration Zoe felt after casting her spell slowly diminished through Wednesday. This is my friend Lolly's partner, she thought; kind, vulnerable Lolly who wouldn't hurt a fly. But Ray's interested in *me*, exciting Ray with those dangerous blue eyes. Then again there's Brandon, my own Brandon.

By Thursday afternoon she was in a moither of uncertainty. The spell was romantic, it made her feel powerful; but this was reality. Shall I phone, she thought, cancel the whole thing? Somehow the arrangement, once made, seemed to have a pull of its own. She drove out fast through the lanes.

The Hollies was a large Victorian house. Ray's car was already in the drive. She drew in behind, switched off the engine, leaving her hands gripping the steering wheel. She checked herself in the mirror. I've come this far, she thought, and got out. Two steps up to the imposing front door. An elaborate knocker. She took a deep breath and knocked twice. The sound echoed down the hall.

Perhaps he hadn't heard. She could tell him she'd come, but he hadn't answered. With the relief of an excuse she turned to go.

The door swung open.

'Zoe.' Ray's greeting was a low rumble, an acknowledgement. When she hesitated, he reached for her hand, and led her inside. She was tense, but the door closed behind her. Decisively. They were private. Nobody knows, she thought.

He kissed her.

*

The Friday morning post brought a white, official-looking A5 envelope. Brandon tore it open. 'We are pleased to inform you...'

'Zoe!' he yelled. 'I've got it! I've got it!'

'What, dear?' Zoe called lightly from the kitchen, clearing the breakfast things.

'The Brighton job! Deputy Head of English! I can't believe it. They didn't give anything away. This is fantastic!'

'Brilliant! Well done. But we must hurry. Talk in the car.'

Brandon bustled about with his briefcase. As he opened the front door, the February air suddenly seemed to smell of spring. In the car he rattled off more details about the job and the school, aware that neither he nor Zoe was saying anything about the commute to Brighton, or any other implications. The pleasure of telling his current boss to stuff it filled his mind.

They parked the car. Zoe gave him a peck on the cheek, said brightly, 'Such good news. Have a really great day,' and headed off to the admin block.

That evening Brandon bought a bottle of his favourite Australian red and opened it as soon as they got in. He was still buoyed up by his success, and took a little while to notice Zoe's calm, slightly abstracted manner. She had her feet tucked in her nest chair, eyes wandering round the room.

Brandon uncrossed his legs and leant forward out of his leather chair.

'Everything all right, Zoe? You seem a bit subdued.'

'Oh, I'm fine, thanks. Really. It's just that I've got a few things on my mind.'

'Penny for them?' asked Brandon.

Zoe sighed. 'Oh dear. This is difficult. I've meant to talk to you for some time, but it hasn't felt right. With you getting the job, I s'pose it changes things.'

Brandon gripped his wine glass with both hands, and waited.

'This is the thing...' She hesitated. 'Look, I've been seeing more of Ray. I'm sure you've felt something. You and me – we've been passing like ships in the night recently, haven't we?'

'Hmpf,' Brandon grunted. 'I know we've been a bit off with each other, but

I didn't realise... Thought it was just a bad patch.' He began to digest what Zoe was saying. 'How long has this been going on?'

'Not long. But long enough to convince me we've drifted too far apart to go back.' She paused. 'I think we've just got to face it, haven't we? I'm afraid it's over between you and me, darling.'

Brandon slumped back in his chair, breathing heavily. A silence settled between them. Eventually he took a sip of wine. What he wanted to say was, 'Zoe, I can't accept this. We have a good life together. We've shared great times in the morris. Think of our special holidays. We've got reliable jobs, we love this flat,' but the words just wouldn't come. He looked up, and simply said, 'I can't believe you're just pushing our whole relationship aside. Our whole lives! I still love you. I want *you*, dammit.'

Zoe flinched, lost for words. She dared not raise her eyes to Brandon's face. Then she took a deep breath.

'Oh Brandon, I'm sorry. We should have talked before. I don't want to hurt you, but things have gone too far. I'm sorry,' she repeated, realising how inadequate the words sounded.

Another tense silence stretched between them, Brandon gazing at Zoe, Zoe looking down and rubbing her toes.

Brandon broke it. 'We need time. Promise me you'll give me time – give us time. Can't just dismiss... Don't do anything for now. Please.'

Zoe looked up. Slowly, she nodded, aware of a wave of relief at escaping more of the charged exchange. She felt touched by Brandon's declaration, but her mind was already rolling away.

'Yes. Right. Yes.' She got up. 'Hard to say any more, just now, isn't it? I know this has come as a shock.'

Brandon snorted. 'Too bloody right it has.' He didn't know what to do with himself. He daren't let his thoughts move towards Ray. Ray, of all people! How could she?

Zoe moved towards the kitchen. 'I think I'll go round and see Louise,' she said over her shoulder. Louise was an old schoolfriend, never a favourite of Brandon's.

'Ok. Yes. I guess I'll probably just stay in.' He felt rooted to his chair.

After the front door closed, he put his head in his hands. 'Oh God, what now, what now?' he muttered, clenching his fists, leaving his wine untouched, with one low light left on in the darkening room.

Chapter 12:
Second Corners

Brandon waited. The routines of work carried him along, and the February days trudged by in a slow tunnel, to be got through buried deep in warm coats against the sleet and penetrating cold. He and Zoe were locked in a stalemate, their conversation at home skating over the surface. He had moved back into their bed, but they kept their corners, Zoe politely but firmly refusing his occasional attempts to show physical affection. She declined his offer not to take up the Brighton job. His frustration fermented.

At practice one night, he told Lolly about the new job.

'Congratulations,' she said, though her heart sank. 'You must be pleased – it's a vote of confidence, given all the competition. Will you commute?'

'I think so,' said Brandon, very subdued. 'At least until I'm properly settled in, but it won't be for a few months yet...' He sighed. The new job, the commuting, somewhere to stay – what did it matter? He felt his life was in ruins. He found Lolly looking intently at his impassive face.

'It's the change you want, though, isn't it?' She tried to be cheerful.

'Oh, I'll be happy to escape Maywood. People always bitching. Grumble grumble grumble.'

The conversation petered out, so many things left unsaid between them.

The side was planning to dance out on a Friday evening in a couple of weeks. Hannah wanted to get everyone moving, and prepare for the season. There was a good pub at Mannerscombe, a village with a small green, and though it would be dark, it was fairly well lit outside. Larksea danced there once or twice a year, and got a good reception from the locals, as well as some of the wealthier newcomers to the village. Alex was keen to put two new dances through their paces.

Ray, meanwhile, was looking at flats. He wanted to have something attractive to show Zoe before he broached the idea of moving in together. Two bedrooms on the seafront, or a large old place overlooking the park that could mean space for Naomi too? Perhaps he should outline the plan, visit several properties, then let her choose. The spice that guilt added to their clandestine meetings didn't pall, exactly, but he wanted to see more of Zoe, and was impatient to move on.

'At least it's dry,' said Hannah, as she and Alex arrived for the Mannerscombe stand. The evening was cool, not yet spring, but there was a sweetness to the country air. The landlord had cleared a good space in front of the pub, and was offering a reduction on jugs of beer. Seven for seven thirty, Hannah had said, but there was an infectious thank-God-it's-Friday atmosphere and Alex didn't manage to rally the side till nearly eight o'clock.

'Any twelve up for the coming on dance,' he called over the chatter. Most of the side had turned out, and he wasn't choosing dancers till they tried out the new ones. Over twenty of the locals trooped out to watch.

Lolly, Pete Kershaw and little Steve struck up 'Drive the Cold Winter Away,' and the two knots of dancers either side of the space stopped milling around, stirred by the familiar call of the tune. Here we go, thought Alex, caught up in the anticipation. He watched as Luke and Sarah stepped towards each other, smiling face to face, excited to be the first out. This was a good idea, he nodded to himself. Spring just around the corner. The morris is waking up.

Zoe and Lolly found themselves opposite each other in 'Constant Billy' Bampton, an old favourite so familiar they could blow away the winter cobwebs and relax into the performance. Lolly glanced across the set and raised her eyebrows; Zoe's response was a toss of her head and a discreet thumbs up sign. She was determined to make a good public display, and as they saluted each other in the first figure she met Lolly's eyes with a broad performance smile. Underneath, she was wondering how much Lolly knew. She didn't think Ray had said anything, but... Lolly, for her part, focussed on synchronising her movements to Zoe's, trying to lose herself in the rhythm of the dance, but her suspicions meant she couldn't meet Zoe's eyes as they circled in the whole gyp.

Towards the end of the stand, Alex called six up for 'Bobby and Joan'

Fieldtown. He hadn't nominated dancers, and by chance it was six men who formed up.

Brandon was feeling listless, and he hadn't been in much of a dancing mood, but the thought of a vigorous stick dance appealed. He had been keeping an eye on Ray, but Ray was on his best behaviour, chaffing with Phil and Len and their cronies, with some over-hearty laughter.

As they shuffled on to dance, Brandon was at number five, and suddenly there was Ray at number six. Damn, thought Brandon, I don't want to be anywhere near this man. But it was too late to change position – or drop out – now. They glanced at each other in the once-to-yourself high clash, and Brandon felt an electric tingle down his wrist from the force of Ray's blow. Sod you, he thought, and threw himself into the stepping of the foot up.

In the first chorus Brandon twisted with his back fully facing Ray, holding his stick high and horizontal as Alex had taught them. Down came Ray's stick with more strength than usual, and Brandon replied with equal force. It was as if they were testing the sticks to destruction.

The whole set was sticking exuberantly, but when it came to the third chorus, Brandon really let rip. The yellow sodium lights down the front of the pub were bright, and the street lamps made pools along the pavement, but the area between them was less well lit. Ray was in the shadow and his stick wasn't horizontal enough, and when Brandon's strike came down at an angle, it thwacked Ray's fingers and slid straight down, hitting him hard on the side of the head.

Ray let out an anguished yelp and staggered, dropped to one knee, then rolled sideways. It took a moment for the others to register what had happened, and there was a syncopated clatter as the chorus disintegrated. Johnny Rendell was instantly down by Ray's side, holding his shoulder.

'Ray! You all right? Ray!' he called urgently. The rest of the side crowded round.

Ray was hunched up with his hands to his head. There was blood oozing between his right fingers.

'First aid box! Has the pub got a first aid box?' called Johnny.

'One in my car!' yelled Carol, and scurried away.

Brandon stood, appalled. What have I done? he thought.

'Take deep breaths,' Johnny told Ray. 'Now, can you sit up?' After a few moments, he lifted Ray's shoulders, and Carol was there with a bandage. The wound looked a mess, with streaks of blood down Ray's neck, his hair glistening darkly round the cut. He felt groggy.

'Right. Casualty. Now,' said Johnny as he wound the bandage round. Lolly was by Ray's side, and sat supporting him with her arm round his waist.

'I'll come,' volunteered Alex. 'Can't go on with the stand now.'

After a few minutes, with members of the side coming over, registering the shock, they managed to manoevre a tottering Ray over to his car. Brandon caught up with them.

'Sorry, Ray, sorry. I don't know what happened. Such bad luck.' It was doubtful if Ray heard him.

Zoe was with the others, offering to accompany them, but Johnny and Alex were clearly in control. She came round to the driver's window. Lolly looked very pale.

'Please phone me the moment there's any news. Please!' Her voice was thick with emotion.

'I will, I will,' Lolly murmured, and turned to look at Ray, slumped beside Johnny on the back seat. 'Ready?' she asked.

Johnny nodded, and she eased the car into the road. The side watched it disappear into the distance and stood in small groups, several shaking their heads, wondering how it could have happened.

Spring

Spring

Chapter 13:
On the Spot and Change

'It was bloody deliberate,' snarled Ray.

The morning after the stand, Lolly had taken Naomi to Saturday swimming club, while Ray slept in. Now she took him a cup of tea upstairs, and sat on the bed beside him. He had two stitches and a spectacular bruise down the side of his head, as well as swollen fingers. She bit her lip. I'll have to allow him to get it out of his system, she thought, feeling tired after the hospital drama and the effort of reassuring Naomi over breakfast.

Ray ranted on. 'If there's any lasting damage, I'm going to sue him. He could see perfectly well.'

Diplomacy, thought Lolly, struggling with her divided loyalties. 'Darling, it was a stick dance. Weren't you all going at it a bit? The set looked really together and, well, energetic, to say the least.'

'You should have seen his face. If that was an accident, I'm a Dutchman.'

Lolly continued to try and soothe him, alarmed herself by the turn of events. She had answered calls and phoned round most of the morris to reassure them that he hadn't been kept in overnight, and though no-one had said anything against Brandon, that didn't stop the niggling question: had his feelings got the better of him? There were so many uncertainties.

Ray rested over the weekend, took the day off on Monday, and despite his outward groans and self-pity, he felt sufficiently recovered to attend practice that night. Everyone welcomed him, made a gratifying fuss of him, and wanted to hear the details. The stitches did look like something out of the London Dungeon, and the bruise was picturesquely yellow and purple. Lolly had talked him out of threatening to lay charges against Brandon, but he was still smouldering with suspicion and resentment when Brandon approached.

'Ray, I can't tell you how sorry I am this has happened. I wish it had been me instead.'

Ray grunted. He was aware the side were listening, and tried hard to sound placatory.

'These things happen, I suppose. But I tell you what. If there's any lasting damage, I'm going to claim. The side's got insurance, hasn't it, Hannah?'

Hannah's face was full of serious concern. 'Yes, we have got the proper protection against this kind of accident, and so on. But of course I hope – we all hope – that you'll make a complete recovery, Ray. So unfortunate.'

Conversations turned around accidents people knew about. Len told them about a man from Kent who had his baldricks snagged by an impatient passing car, and was dragged along and got his ankle crushed. Several people knew of sticks shattering spectacularly, one causing an eye injury to a member of the public. Phil Clothier kept repeating that they should all wear their hats for stick dances. The previous year the side had agreed not to wear them for stick dances as they got in the way. Luke, out of earshot, muttered to Pete Kershaw, 'Can't be that bad if Ray feels up to coming here tonight, can it. In some ways he had it coming to him, don't you think?'

Alex started the practice, with Ray sitting on the sidelines. He looked solemn and knew he was drawing attention to himself.

Next day, Ray phoned Zoe. She was cooing with sympathy. 'Actually, I'm better this morning,' he said. 'No headache. And it's great to lie in bed and let the world bustle away. You know, I think he meant to hit me. He certainly wanted to.'

'I wasn't close enough to see clearly. You all seemed pretty lively towards the end of the stand.' She sighed. 'Oh Ray, I can't believe this has happened. If it was deliberate, it'd be so out of charcater for Brandon.'

'Even so, I think it shows his real feelings. And I can't bear the thought of you having to put up with that kind of resentment.'

'That's really sweet of you, thanks. Well, we're civil enough to each other at home.'

'But it's horrible. Look, it's hard to talk on the phone, I know. Can you meet me on Friday? I'm planning to go into the office to prepare for next week. Can you meet me there after work?'

'I don't see why not. I could pretend to be a client!'

Ray put on his best estate agent's voice. 'Marvellous. Well, Mrs Corfield, please come this way. I think we'll have something interesting to show you.' They both laughed, Ray enjoying the hidden knowledge that he really did have three flats lined up.

On the Friday, Zoe was at the estate agent's by four- thirty.

'Ah yes, Mrs Corfield,' said the bright young receptionist, very front-of-house, with elegantly streaked blonde hair and dark pink lipstick. 'Mr Jenner is expecting you. Please come through.' She knocked at the rear door, which had a large mirror in it.

'Come!' called Ray. Zoe thought he was playing the alpha male.

'Here's your four thirty, Mr Jenner,' simpered the receptionist. Zoe didn't quite like the way the woman looked at Ray, as if she wasn't used to addressing him formally. She noticed it was a two-way mirror.

As soon as the door closed, Ray got up, came round his desk and embraced Zoe. For a moment she felt awkward, changing so quickly from public to private, but then returned his kiss warmly.

'No point in hanging around,' said Ray. He picked up a folder of house details and ushered Zoe into the front office.

'I'll take those keys, Annette,' he said, and she brought three sets over to him. 'Lock up at five- thirty, won't you. I'll come back later myself. See you Monday.'

'Yes,sir. It'll be a relief to have you back.' Her face was bright but enigmatic. Ray swept Zoe out of the office.

'What bijou residence are we "reviewing" this time?' asked Zoe with a knowing smile.

'Aha, you'll see,' said Ray. 'Actually, it's a flat on the seafront.'

'Not the kind of mansion I'm used to, Mr Jenner,' Zoe replied archly.

They made love passionately in the sparsely furnished flat. At one point Ray said, 'Ouch! Be gentle with me...' Afterwards, they lay quietly for some time, letting the glow linger on. As they nuzzled together, Ray could feel her eyelashes just brushing his shoulder. Eventually he sat up. 'Come into the front room,' he said. While Zoe was in the bathroom, he went into the main living room and opened the curtains onto the sea view. He quickly took a bottle of champagne and two glasses out of his case, and set them on a coffee table with two armchairs on either side, in front of some full length balcony windows.

'I say!' Zoe took in the view, and the champagne. With a sibilant chorus girl giggle she said, 'You do know how to show a girl a good time.'

'I want to, I want to,' he said, and they beamed at each other as he opened the champagne with a satisfying pop.

'Cheers, Zoe. Here's to us.'

Zoe met his gaze, and held it. 'Yes, to *us*,' she said, raising her glass.

As the dusk gathered, a soft violet over the sea, Ray outlined his plans and his hopes. Zoe listened, watching his bruised face intently, absorbing his seriousness. The glamour of the moment started to fade for her. Ray talked on, unaware that with each emphatic declaration, he was pushing Zoe further from his carefully constructed romantic scene into the splintered mirrors of herself.

She sat back, and gazed at the sea. Do I really want to live with him? she wondered, actually move in with him, abandon Brandon, maybe even have to take on Naomi? For a moment she was back in her safe flat with the old Brandon, and yearned to return to that simple happiness. Then a part of her protested. That was yesterday's Brandon. Now they were trapped with each other, and he had lost his certainty for her, even if he was jealous enough to hit Ray. She found that his displays of affection were well meant but didn't move her. She thought: I could have a new life with this magnetic man, sitting here full of ardour and admiration for me, making a new place, moving on.

She realised Ray had stopped talking and was waiting, looking intently at her, his eyes fierce with longing. She knew she must respond.

'It's a wonderful vision,' she said softly. 'Daring. A very big step.'

'We can make it work.' Ray's voice was tight.

She leant towards him, and gently took his swollen hand. 'I need a little longer, darling. It's exciting, but it's a lot to take in. Can you bear with me for a bit?'

'I want to be with you, Zoe. Everything else is... secondary.'

She kissed him then, feeling his commitment, but her mind was fluctuating. She surfaced into a more practical present.

'Let's see the other flats. You've been to such trouble.' She could hear Brandon's words echoing: 'Promise me you'll give me time, give us time,' he'd said. She looked at Ray directly. 'Promise me you won't say anything to Lolly yet.'

Ray sighed. 'If I must. But don't spin it out for long. I couldn't bear it. I love you.'

Zoe inhaled sharply. It was what she wanted to hear. 'Ray,' was all she could say, and hugged him briefly.

'Come on, let's finish the champers,' Ray said. He poured the glasses and slowly drew the curtains.

Chapter 14:
Whole Hey

FRIDAY EVENING

Zoe got home around eight – thirty, having texted Brandon that she was meeting up with Louise after work.

He didn't get up to greet her, but he didn't want to end up with another strained conversation either, so all he said was, 'Shall I phone for a takeaway?'

'Oh, not tonight, thanks. There's that chicken left and I'm not hungry anyway.'

Brandon was determined to try and keep things on an even keel. 'Would you prefer to go out for a drink?' he suggested. 'There's that live jazz down at the Brahms and Liszt. It was good last month.'

'Tempting, but I'm soggy-end-of-the-week rather than fired up. Nice thought, but I'll stay in. Don't let me stop you though. You'll know quite a few there.'

She was keen to match his considerate tone. 'I think I'll watch *Boardroom* at nine.' It was a programme that Brandon tolerated but wouldn't have chosen.

'Ah, okay. Well then, would you mind if I went? I'm only in the mood for a bag of chips myself.'

'No, you go. Enjoy. See you later.'

Brandon went straight out.

SATURDAY

Next morning they dozed a while before Brandon got up to make a cup of tea. He padded into the warm kitchen in his boxers. While the kettle was boiling, he noticed Zoe's carrier bag on the floor. It was open at the top and his eye immediately caught the logo of Ray's firm on some papers poking out of the top. He checked himself momentarily, but the urge to know more took him over, and he pulled out the papers.

Details of three flats, all local. The kettle clicked off. Brandon stood, staring at Ray's name, and snatched his breath in a surge of anger. He grabbed the papers.

Zoe was sitting up waiting for her tea. Brandon threw the details onto her lap. Her eyes narrowed. She looked up.

'What's this then?' Brandon stared down at her, his chest heaving. A silence settled between them.

Zoe carefully pulled her hair back from her forehead. She sighed. 'Come and sit down. I'll explain.'

'That's where you were yesterday evening, wasn't it? You were out with Ray.'

'I was with Ray, yes. He suggested looking at some flats...'

'And why the hell would he do that?'

'Calm down, Brandon. I said I'd explain. Please come and sit down.'

He didn't move. 'Explain away.'

'Look, Ray was just being sensible, thinking ahead. If you were to move to Brighton...'

'You mean the pair of you have been scheming behind my back. When I asked you to give us more time I didn't mean... I didn't mean more time to get into bloody bed with him. You've been sleeping with him, haven't you?'

'Brandon, I...'

'I've been waiting, hoping we could patch things up, find each other again. You've taken the law into your own hands. Waiting till you've set things up. I can't believe... you've been... so two-faced.'

Zoe was riled, and abandoned any attempt to pacify him. 'No I haven't. It's not two-faced to look ahead. In case things didn't work out for us. And have they? You've been waiting to have a go at me for ages. You'll probably move to Brighton anyway.'

Brandon was speechless for a moment, his face flushed, his fists clenched. Then he spoke slowly, his lips tight, leaning towards her.

'I even offered not to go! I can't believe this. You've been calculating all along. No wonder you said it was – what was it? "too important for me to give Brighton up." I'd be out of your way.'

They stared at each other. Brandon took a step back.

'Things have gone far enough, Zoe. You said it was over. I hoped against hope, but no. I've been a fool. You sneaked off. That's it. Finished.' He turned sharply and went to the bathroom.

Zoe pulled her knees up and rocked herself. The papers slithered to the floor. She was angry, but also stirred by Brandon's anger; he had looked so strong. Had he been right earlier? Could they patch up their marriage, find each other again, even now? she wondered.

Brandon slammed the door and jumped down the stairs two at a time. He stomped off towards the seafront, seething. Fool, fooling yourself, fool, he kept repeating in his head.

The sea was choppy, waves hissing on the shingle, the sky overcast but with a strange silvery light on the horizon. He wanted a storm, and strode along, till some of his energy was spent; then he stopped, leaning on the promenade rail, and watched the sea as his breathing quietened, and his thoughts began to circle again. How much does Lolly know about this, he wondered. Would she be too loyal to say anything, go on playing a waiting game like me? He felt a tenderness towards her and their painful situation. No, damnit, he thought, why should Ray get away with it? And I want to know if Lolly's aware of any of this. It's not right for her to be kept in the dark. He took out his mobile.

Answerphone. Brandon nearly put his mobile away, but then he blurted, 'Lolly, it's Brandon. Sorry to bother you. It's Saturday ten-thirty. Could you phone me back? It's important.' He walked on, scarcely noticing what direction he was taking. He began to think he should delay doing anything till he was calmer, when he was startled by his ring tones. It was Lolly.

'Brandon, hello. Got your call. Are you all right?' The concern in her voice made him swallow hard. His hand was shaking.

'Have you got a moment? Thing is, I've had a big row with Zoe.'

'Oh. I'm so sorry. Erm, I'm in Tesco's at the moment. But go on, tell me.'

Now he was speaking to her, Brandon was in too much of a whirl of emotion to stop, so it all poured out about finding the flat details, and Ray and Zoe visiting them.

He paused. 'Hello?...hello? Are you still there?'

'Yes, sorry. It's just...' Lolly's voice sounded strained. 'I didn't know any of this. Why would they.... but you mean...'

'Yes, I'm afraid I do mean that. I wasn't sure how much you knew. Zoe and I, well, we've been on the rocks for some time. I've told her it's over.'

'Oh Brandon, that's awful. You must be feeling terrible.'

'Sorry to dump it on you like this. Look, you must finish your shopping. I just needed to know if...'

'Yes. I see. Erm, okay. P'raps we can talk more later.'

'Of course. Of course. Sorry.'

'It's all right. Bye for now.'

Brandon sat down heavily on a bench, feeling numb. Should I have done that? he wondered. For her part, Lolly was walking round the shelves, staring blankly at labels, stunned. Must finish the shopping, just finish the shopping...

By the time she got home, she knew she must confront Ray. Hannah had taken Naomi swimming with Steve; she could have it out with Ray privately.

He came into the kitchen as she was stacking the packets. She knew she'd falter if she didn't plunge straight in.

'I've had a phone call from Brandon. He says you've been looking at flats with Zoe. Is this true?'

Ray hesitated, calculating quickly. 'Well, yes, but look, whoa! Don't read too much into it. Seems as if Brandon may move to Brighton, and they could buy a smaller place to help him pay his way there.'

'You mean Zoe's intending to stay here without him?' Ray was trying to pick up some of the packets, but Lolly was facing him across the table.

'Look at me, Ray. There's more to this, isn't there? Zoe's been awkward with me for weeks, and Brandon says...'

'Brandon says, Brandon says! Why do you always support that man? You know he's got it in for me.'

'Has he? Are you sure? Why?' Lolly felt a fireball rising inside her. Anger, doubt, mistrust, and her instinct came together. 'Why d'you think he's got it in for you, Ray? Answer me. I want the truth. Don't you dare fob me off with words. Are you having an affair?'

The directness of the question floored Ray. He sat down. He'd known he'd have to face things sooner or later. Better now, he thought, if Brandon had already found out. Zoe must have told him. Keeping the thought of Zoe in mind, he closed his eyes, and nodded.

'I didn't want it to be like this, Lolly. I'm sorry.'

'So you're not denying it.'

'No, I'm not. I didn't want to hurt you. Yes. You deserve the truth. The fact is, I've fallen in love with Zoe.'

Lolly found her hands clamped round the tins. She turned and put them away. Ray watched her intently. She turned back and looked at him, her face impassive, shook her head, and walked into the living room. Ray followed her.

'Lolly, I know this is a shock for you, but can't we talk it through...'

'Not now, Ray. Not now.'

'There's a lot more to say.'

'Yes there is.' Lolly was suddenly vehement. 'A lot more. But not now. Leave me alone.'

Ray had not encountered Lolly so steely before. I'll make a cup of coffee and take it in to her, he thought, and went into the kitchen. Just as he was about to pour the water, he heard the front door close firmly.

Lolly knew she must be on her own. The pricking in her eyes told her she was going to weep. She walked purposefully towards the park, and found a quiet corner. She let go, tears first, then sobs. As they subsided, her thoughts returned.He's been living a lie with me, and I've just let us go on. Her anger turned to Zoe. She's really betrayed me. Friend! Ha! And with Ray, of all the men she could have chosen. She felt utterly abandoned, flattened, and unloved.

She looked up and saw someone coming. Pull yourself together, she murmured to herself, and blew her nose. Naomi will be back within the hour. I must be there for her. What about Brandon? Poor Brandon. But no. I'm not up to speaking to him yet.

She couldn't decide what to do. In the end, she texted him. 'It's true,' was all she said, and made her way back home, deep in thought.

Ray, meanwhile, phoned Zoe. They had a rapid, intense exchange, and agreed they must talk. They arranged Sunday lunchtime.

The rest of Saturday passed in an uneasy, artificial calm in both households.

SUNDAY

On Sunday morning, Lolly busied herself round the house. Her silence was getting Ray down, and when he eventually asked her how she was feeling, she felt too bruised to begin a conversation. He said, 'Well, if you don't mind, I think I'd like to go and see Zoe.' So much for building bridges, she thought. A little later she phoned Hannah and arranged to go round with Naomi in the afternoon.

Ray drove Zoe to Mannerscombe. 'A pub with memories,' he grinned, rubbing the side if his head ruefully. His bruises were still quite marked. For her part, Zoe was going over her morning with Brandon. She had tried to be placatory, but he stonewalled her, and she realised, with a wry twist to her tangled emotions, that she was not going to be able to get past his anger. Being rejected was something new to her, and Ray's certainty was very reassuring. As they left Larksea, he suggested they stop in Marfield Lane on the way, to be able to talk openly.

Rolling woodland and a distant grey-green line of glittering sea greeted them. He reached rather clumsily over the handbrake to take her hand, and she leant against him. They stayed that way without speaking for some time. Ray spoke first.

'Zoe, I've got things to say. I don't know how to get through this without you. Without knowing we can be together. I thought we'd have longer, but it's all come to a head so quickly. Can I tell you what I've been thinking?'

She squeezed his hand, and nodded.

*

When Ray got in, he was itching to speak, but Lolly whispered, 'Talk once Naomi's in bed,' and they got through the evening meal with an appearance of normality. Ray helped Naomi prepare for school and managed not to rush things.

'Kitchen's best,' said Lolly, closing the door as they finished the washing up. She knew Ray wanted 'a serious talk,' and faced him across the table.

'This is really hard, Lolly. But now we all know the score, I think it's time to get things straight.'

Lolly bit back her impulse to snort 'Straight?! Who are you kidding?' and simply folded her arms. She had come a long way since yesterday, and was seeing Ray in a new, harsher light.

He cleared his throat.

'The thing is, one of those flats I saw with Zoe on Friday is available in a month. That sort of gives us a timescale, and time to adjust as well. What I'd like to do is to move in with Zoe, and she agrees.'

Does she indeed? thought Lolly. Time for who to adjust? She fought to control her voice. 'That's not long, Ray. I can't stop you, and to be honest, now, I don't want to. It's Naomi we've got to think about.'

'Oh I know, I know. Of course I hope she'll want to stay with her Dad. Another upheaval for her, but...'

'Yes. And what does Zoe say?' Lolly was incisive.

'She agrees, but says it should be Naomi's choice.'

'Too damn right it should. And it's too sudden. If you're really set on this move, we must break it to her gently. Maybe in stages. You know, something like "Daddy is going away for a bit but will see lots of you." Put yourself in her shoes.'

'All right, all right. This is painful for me too, you know.'

Lolly felt a flash of anger. She glared at Ray. Her own feeling was that Naomi should stay in her familiar surroundings, at least till any new arrangements were more settled, and Ray had made certain she knew he still loved her. For the moment, Lolly bided her time.

Ray stumbled on. 'We can certainly go softly softly, give ourselves time to work out some practicalities.'

'Yes, we *will* wait.' Lolly spat the words out. She got up, pushed her chair under the table, and went into the living room.

Ray realised the conversation was terminated.

Monday

Monday morning, and the working week took them into their separate lives; Naomi and Brandon to school, Lolly to the shop, Ray and Zoe to their different offices. Each felt the temporary relief of having to cope with the day-to-day, though their emotions churned on underneath.

Ray and Lolly had their usual babysitter coming, and neither wanted to miss going to morris, awkward though it might be. To Lolly's dismay, there was no Brandon at practice. Zoe breezed in, giving his apologies – he was feeling a bit off colour, she claimed – and the three of them managed to go about practice without apparent tension.

At the end of the evening, Hannah had a list of admin to get through. She waved her notebook to try and quell the usual hubbub.

The side were planning a day of dance on Easter Saturday. Larksea's rivals along the coast, Mugsborough, had made enquiries about having a shared stand, and asked if they could bring a small group of French visitors, who would be over from Dieppe. Hannah proposed they make a whole day of it, and host a supper and informal ceilidh in the evening. She got an enthusiastic response, with plenty of offers to bring food and prepare the hall, and scribbled notes of all the arrangements she would have to make. Carol volunteered to organise the hall and food, and Charlie said he's get The Anchor to do the bar, but the side could run to a small keg of beer and a couple of boxes of wine to welcome the visitors. There was a real buzz; the season was getting under way.

Martin signalled to Hannah and cut across the chatter. 'Folks, shush, if I may... I'd like my mate Gary to be a fellow Gull for the day. He's been to a few of our stands, and he knows not to get in the way of the dancers. Got to know exactly what you're doing if you're squawking in and out of a hey.' He threw in a gull squawk for good measure. 'It could be fun. If it doesn't work out, just say so, and no harm done.' He got a cheerful approval.

During the meeting, Lolly quietly left with her mobile to seek the privacy of the ladies. She had thought she could have at least a quick conversation with Brandon. The need to speak to him had been growing in her the whole day. Now all she could do was snatch a few whispered words out of sight of the others.

Brandon's voice was very low.

'Brandon it's me, Lolly. I'm at practice. I've only got a minute. Are you all right?'

There was a pause. 'Not really, no. Just got to keep going.'

'I really want to see you. Sorry to be abrupt, but can you come to the shop at five-thirty tomorrow? I hoped you'd be here tonight.'

'Couldn't face the whole situation. Yes, I can do that. I'd like to do that. See you at five-thirty.'

Lolly returned unobtrusively to the meeting and sat near Ray on the floor.

Tuesday

Another day of waiting. It was late March, overcast and wintry as Brandon and Lolly dragged themselves slowly through the day. Brandon was very prompt, and Lolly tried hard to be bright when they met. He suggested a cafe, but they closed at six and it felt too early for a pub, so they set off for the seafront under the lowering sky. There was an old shelter at the end of the prom where they could be secluded.

After a few pleasantries, Brandon said, 'I really didn't mean to hit him, you know. When I got the Brighton job Zoe pretty well admitted there was something going on, but it wasn't till last Saturday that it all came out. Those flat details. I was in two minds about telling you.'

'I'm glad you did. I've had my suspicions for weeks. At least I know where I am now. He told me he'd fallen in love with Zoe.'

'What a mess. How are you feeling?'

'Resigned, sort of. Angry at first. Still am. He's been two-faced, really sly.'

'God yes. I said much the same to Zoe. You know,' he grinned wanly, 'I'm glad I hit him. Maybe I knew underneath.'

'And you, Brandon?' She glanced at him. 'Any idea where you go from here?'

Brandon broke his stride, gathering his thoughts. 'I've only a few weeks to go before the new job starts. I had a long chat with some friends on Sunday. They said I could stay there for a bit. I just don't want to be at the flat with Zoe now.'

'Oh dear. It's all a bit dramatic, isn't it?' said Lolly, galvanised by the thought that Brandon might move away. 'I mean, it may not last between them, don't you think?'

'Hmm. It feels to me as if they've decided. Finding a flat together's a pretty clear statement, I'd say. No, I've been holding my breath for long enough. I need to make a break.'

They were nearing the shelter. Lolly glanced back; the prom was as bleak and bare as an airstrip.

Once they were settled, they both looked blankly out to sea. The waves were breaking restlessly. A thought was brewing in Lolly's mind. She mustered her courage and turned to Brandon.

'Where to begin? I mean, there's Naomi to consider for a start. Ray says he'll let her choose, but I feel strongly she needs to stay where she is. But be near her father too. My thought is, I mean might you consider...' Lolly went on quickly, 'As a temporary thing, if you do move out, would you object to Ray staying with Zoe for a bit? Until it's more settled. This getting a flat business, it's so definite, such a departure...'

Brandon recoiled. Let that bastard into his own home? No. But the old home was falling apart. He was going to leave it, his own choice. He had already been turning over the implications, the financial ones not least, in this anguish of break-up. Now he was sitting with Lolly, and it all looked different; the timescale was dim and messy. He struggled with all the uncertainties, trying to fit the pieces of the jigsaw together.

Lolly was watching him closely, fearful that she had offended him. Her suggestion had been on the spur of the moment as she reacted to the feeling that too much was happening too quickly. She sat, rigid with apprehension.

Brandon continued to ride a tight knot of conflicting thoughts and emotions, but suddenly a movement leapt out, a shock reaction to the picture of Ray living in his flat: if Ray can play at house-swapping, why can't I do the same? I'm the one looking for a place. He allowed himself to think the unthinkable: perhaps I could go and stay at Lolly's.

Lolly broke the silence. 'Sorry, Brandon. I wasn't thinking straight. I can see that wouldn't be...'

He saw her frown, saw her delicacy of feeling for him, let himself look at her. Gently, he held his hand up.

'No, you're right, I can see where you're coming from. Mind you, it's the last thing I would have thought of!' He broke off as a series of images invaded his thoughts, Ray sitting in his favourite chair, Ray using his shaving mirror... Ray in his bedroom... He shook his head to dismiss the unwelcome thoughts. 'You'll have to... give me a few minutes.' He felt like a bewildered bear, but after months of Zoe bristling like a cat, the thought of being with Lolly was a haven. His mind cleared. Here was warm, lively, sympathetic Lolly, and she was a lot else besides... A wire of tension in him snapped. This was the woman who had buried her head in his shoulder that January night. He let out an involuntary sigh.

Lolly felt his frustration. 'I'm so sorry, Brandon. That was thoughtless, so stupid of me...' But Brandon leant over, reached out and hugged her, his shoulders shaking. He began to sob. Lolly was taken aback, then after a few moments her heart went out to him, and she reached up and let her hand run over his hair.

Once his shaking subsided, Brandon released her, and fumbled for his handkerchief. He turned fully to face her, and took her hand. She was astonished to hear him chuckle.

'D'you know what's occurred to me?' he sniffed. 'If Ray moves in with Zoe, perhaps I could stay with you for a bit.' He laughed more openly, embarrassed. The world was whirling. Anything seemed possible.

'Ohh,' Lolly stuttered, 'oh...' She squeezed his hand in return, blinking, a slow smile spreading across her face. 'Now that *is* something to think about.' Her words came out in a kind of purr, and they both sat, fuzzy with a growing elation, hardly daring to take their own boldness seriously.

'I suppose we should try and be grown up and think about it,' said Brandon eventually, his voice high and quavering. 'I'm just imagining the look on Zoe's face!'

Like naughty children, they were both suppressing giggles.

'Yes, we'd better sleep on it, don't you think?' Lolly was trying to be serious. Brandon's eyebrows shot up. 'Sleep on it?' he repeated, and they both laughed. 'No, really, we should,' she pleaded with a smile. 'But I like it!'

'I rather like it too! The idea's... growing on me.' Brandon got up. 'Come on, let's go and have a drink. Your hands are freezing.'

He buried her hand in his pocket, and they set off briskly, broad smiles breaking over their faces.

Chapter 15:
Rounds

Brandon phoned Lolly at lunchtime the next day. She nipped into the back yard of the shop.

The lift in his voice was unmistakable. 'I've, erm, slept on it. Not that I needed to, really. It was a good sleep. You still like the idea?'

'Like it? Oh yes. I had a good sleep too. And a better waking up!' Lolly was chirruping.

'Great. I'd like to talk it through with Zoe tonight. You up for telling Ray? Are we rushing things a bit?'

'No, no point in waiting. I really love the idea. I 'spect there must be all sorts of things we haven't thought of, but hey! Let's face them as they come up.' Lolly did a few jig steps in the scruffy yard, oblivious of the unromantic surroundings.

'Good-oh. Text if anything occurs to you. Otherwise, I'll ring you about nine tonight. See how this crazy idea has gone down.'

'If this is crazy, "give me excess of it"!' Lolly was bubbling. 'Perhaps text first, see if either of us is still in the throes. Can't think what I'll say.'

'Me neither,' said Brandon, 'but let it roll. I shan't beat about the bush. Time for some action.'

'*Rather,*' said Lolly. 'Nine tonight it is.'

*

'I've been talking to Brandon,' Lolly announced.

Ray put his can of beer down carefully. They had just settled down in their living room. His defences went up immediately. If she's going to be obstructive, he thought, I'll have to fight.

'This flat business seems a bit, well, complicated. And probably expensive.'

There was something in Lolly's tone. 'We all need time to get used to things.' She knew her nervousness was making her sound like an agony aunt, but she ploughed on. 'I think we need a temporary arrangement. As you want to be with Zoe...' She blinked, swallowed and dived off the deep end. 'As you want to be with Zoe, perhaps you could move in with her for a while. And Brandon could stay here.' The last part came out in a rush.

Ray's hand shot to his mouth. He shook his head in disbelief. Move in with Zoe? Wow! But... but Brandon here? He pulled at the point of his chiselled goatee, eyes wide. Lolly's proposal began to sink in. He reached for his beer.

'You've talked to Brandon about this?' he said eventually, his voice barely under control. The ground was slipping away from under him. 'He's... he's prepared to let this happen?'

'Yes. We talked about it last night. He's asking Zoe what she thinks, now.'

'What about Naomi? I mean, this is really sudden.'

'Well, it's a bit of a temporary try-out, if you agree. So she'd stay here and go on as normal for a bit. Well sort of normal.' Brandon had joked about being a novice at the school run.

'I see. Erm... I need to think about this. I'm not against it, mind, just surprised.' He disappeared into the kitchen.

Lolly sat, rubbing her knees through her jeans. She'd done it! Fingers crossed, she thought, touch wood, pity I'm not religious. She pressed her lips together.

Ray stared, unseeing, out of the kitchen window. This was extraordinary. Would Zoe agree? His heart leapt at the idea. Getting a flat had seemed bold, a stepping out for him and Zoe. But for Lolly to propose... hm. Would Zoe have him at her flat? Then they needn't wait to rent... much less expensive... He didn't want to think too much about Brandon being in his house. What's been going on? He must ask Lolly more about that; but he didn't need to think any longer. He returned to the living room.

'Lolly. I think it could work. If Zoe agrees. Tell me more...'

' ...So you see, if you agree, it could be a workable solution for the time being.' Brandon sat back. He appeared calm, but his hands gripped the side of his chair.

Zoe's mind was reeling. Brandon with Lolly? It was one thing for her and Ray to make a new place, to move on, but for Brandon to move in with... her friend Lolly!

'How long have you been harbouring this?' was all she could think to ask.

'Oh, it's very recent. You and Ray looking for a flat - it made some things clear to me and to Lolly.'

Zoe waited for more explanation. None was forthcoming. She began to consider the possibility. This is embarrassingly neat, she thought. A straight swap? What will people think? She could hear it now, the gossip, malarky in the morris... But Ray, here, yes, minimal upheaval; and we can always have finding a flat as a fallback position. Something in her did not want to agree straight away. But she felt a tingle of excitement.

'Are you sure you want this?' she asked. She couldn't resist trying to probe Brandon's feelings.

He refused to be drawn. 'Yes,' he said tersely. 'We've thought about it.'

The 'we' gave Zoe another flutter of confusion. She felt a twinge of resentment. But if Brandon had any reservations, she couldn't tell. The 'no entry' signs were up.

'I think I'd like a gin and tonic,' she said.

A short while later, Ray was roaring across town to Zoe's. He'd managed not to appear too over-eager as he left Lolly, but a brief word with Zoe on the phone had fired him up. The speed limit had never seemed so slow.

Just as he was walking up to Zoe's flat, suddenly Brandon emerged from the entrance. Their eyes locked, and they both checked, standing still, like two equal and opposite magnetic forces.

Brandon was the first to speak.

'That was quick,' he said, fixing Ray with a straight look.

Ray felt like a guilty schoolboy. 'Yes, I, er, no traffic, green lights,' he blustered.

Brandon dismissed him with a 'hmpf,' and walked away without looking back.

*

At the swimming club on Saturday, Hannah was full of her news about getting a raise and more responsibility at the solicitor's. Lolly found it easier to listen than to say what was on her mind.

'And no additional hours, either! I think I've benefited from those clueless temps the agency has been sending. The last one burst into tears if you suggested anything. And did I tell you about Angie getting a school prize for her recorder? She's actually a pleasure to listen to now.'

Lolly nodded encouragement. She waited till the children were changing afterwards. Then she knew she mustn't delay any longer.

'Hannah, will you and Alex be in this evening? It's just that...'

Hannah was still bubbling on. 'We're off out at eight. Mum's babysitting. Just to the session at the pub. Always good as long as that burk from Brighton doesn't try to hog things. But what's it about? Can we help?'

'Oh, it needn't be for long. It's just that, um, Brandon and I wanted to come and see you both. Won't take long. Can we pop in about seven?'

'Of course you can. Is it about the morris? Something troubling you?'

'Yes and no. A couple of things we want to talk through with you, that's all. Ah, there's Naomi. Got all your things, love?'

Hannah wanted to ask more. Not like Lolly to be mysterious. But Lolly was bright and full of bustle.

'So see you about seven? Sure that's all right?' She called over to Angie. 'Well done with the recorder prize! You'll be playing for Larksea next!' and she hurried Naomi away.

Alex was puzzled. Lolly and Brandon coming together? As he changed for the evening, he kept wondering what they might want – a new dance, a new tradition, even? But why together? The day had been too busy to speculate for long, so he and Hannah had to content themselves with suspicions. Something was going on behind the scenes.

'We wanted you to be the first to know.' Lolly had done most of the talking, sitting rather upright on the edge of Alex and Hannah's old sofa.

'I'm amazed all four of you can be so civilised about it,' said Alex. 'I really hope it all works out. Have you, I mean, found a way to tell Naomi yet?'

'Yes. Ray and I explained it as something that was happening for the time being. Dad will just be staying with Zoe for a bit, sort of thing, and Brandon will be staying with us. Mercifully she didn't ask questions. I don't think she's churned up and emotional, not yet anyway.'

'Difficult for you both. Any thoughts about longer term?' asked Hannah. 'Not easy, I know, but how do you feel, Brandon? It'll be quite a change.'

'I'll do my best. I like Naomi. She's a great kid. And she'll be in her own home. Longer term? I really can't tell. If Naomi chooses to go with Ray, it'll be a big adjustment, especially for Zoe.' Not to mention me, thought Lolly.

'Hm. Well, one thing at a time, I suppose,' said Hannah. 'When's it all going to happen?'

'Tomorrow, actually,' said Brandon, slightly sheepish. 'I'm just going to pack a suitcase and a few work things. Take it from there.'

'I think you're both being very brave,' said Alex. 'Really, I hope it works out. Will you come to morris on Monday?'

'We've discussed it,' said Lolly. 'Bound to be awkward at first. We're going to meet up with Ray and Zoe beforehand and arrive together, then try to practice as normal.'

Brandon nodded. 'It won't be long before it gets out, I bet. But we wanted to tell you in person, before it does.' He looked at Alex. 'Hope it doesn't make any difficulties at the morris.'

'Can't see that it will. As long as you four are at ease with it.' And are you four really at ease with this? thought Alex.

'We mustn't keep you,' said Lolly, acutely aware of what was going on beneath the politeness.

Hannah jumped up, went over to Lolly, and kissed her.

'We're with you, Lolly. Brandon. Just tell us if there's anything we can do.'

'Thanks. You're very...' Lolly's eyes were glistening.

'We'll be here,' said Alex, patting Brandon on the back.

Chapter 16:
Galley Out

Lolly loved the lighter evenings. Now that the clocks had gone forward, she felt catapulted into spring, with the warmer air, the rich scent of wallflowers in people's gardens as she passed; even the dandelions looked cheerful.

That first morris practice hadn't been too bad, she thought. The past week with Brandon had been almost unreal, the ease alongside the excitement, his kindness, the feeling-just-right, the sheer happiness. She was almost skipping her way home. She thought of the way Ray had been over that last weekend, and smiled ruefully; so transparent, now he'd got what he wanted, so considerate, so yes-dear-no-dear.

But this next practice was going to be tricky. Zoe's way of letting people know what was happening had been to talk to Carol, in confidence of course, and Hannah had warned her that the news was all over the side. Shall I duck out for a week? she wondered. But Brandon will be with me. Just put one foot in front of the other, but not in the old depressed way, yes, walk forward. Brandon – yes, Brandon! Is here with me.

They got to practice early, so they could chat to Hannah and Alex and mingle as usual as the side assembled. By the time Ray and Zoe made their entrance, the old scout hall was buzzing like an excited classroom. Zoe was looking severe but handsome, tight black jeans and loose top, her black hair tied back with her favourite turquoise scarf. Everyone was on their best behaviour, though a few eyes were swivelling.

Alex cleared his throat. 'Right. I've sketched out the main dances for the big day with Mugsborough on Saturday.' He held up a list. 'Open to negotiation of course, so the "who's doing what" bit is mostly suggestions. What I want is for everyone to feel confident so we can show 'em! Should be fun. Okay. Coming on dance...'

There was a here-we-go swing to the evening. Amy Kershaw had a spectacular collision with Sarah, normally an occasion for some grumpiness, but tonight it was hilarious, the dress rehearsal nerves dissolving into knockabout. Lolly and

Zoe found themselves on opposite corners for "Bobbing Around." Walk tall, Lolly said to herself as their eyes met, each carefully co-ordinating her movements to the other. Zoe sensed a new confidence in Lolly; she was smiling, and held Zoe's gaze, more in acknowledgement than defiance. Lolly was thinking; no winners or losers here, I can do this, and walked off the set to where her lion king of a Brandon was standing.

On their way home, both Hannah and Alex were pleased with the way practice had gone. 'This mixed side business works, you know,' said Alex, matching his step with Hannah's. 'It's like doubling your resources.'

'It does, it does,' Hannah responded warmly. 'We can nearly always muster a side for any aways, as well as a strong side for anything locally. But I'm glad we've kept a few dances separate. I love doing Maid of the Mill with the women. You blokes can keep Vandalls.'

'Oh we will, we will. Thinking of vandals, how d'you think it's going with our crazy couples? I can't believe it's going to be all sweetness and light.'

'Very early days. This could be the easy part. I wouldn't want to bet on which pair will be happier. Who knows? They've got the glow, now. All we can do is go with that.'

*

Easter Saturday, scudding clouds. A fresh westerly up the Channel blew all the morris ribbons horizontal, and kept the two stands on the promenade quite brisk. There were plenty of holidaymakers about, but they didn't linger to watch more than one dance. Mugsborough were on good form, with strong teams for both their men's and women's sides, making for a competitive edge to the dancing. Larksea opened with one double set of Shepherd's Hey Bampton, then it was the turn of the Mugsborough men, doing their different version of Bampton with noticeably high capers in The Webley, followed by an elegant performance of Sweet Jenny Jones from the women.

Alex set up two dances for Larksea next, with exaggerated but good-humoured complaints from Mugsborough that if you must go and mix up your men and your women, one dance should count as a whole turn, and so why couldn't they follow straight away, call yourselves hosts, hogging the limelight... Jeers from Mugsborough, cheers from Larksea as the second Larksea set started up quickly.

The two Gulls were everywhere, pecking playfully at Mugsborough dancers, capturing one pretty girl and wafting her away in folded wings. Now one was perched on the railings, apparently having an argument with a particularly large herring gull, bold enough not to flap away. The other Gull was making a show of going through a rubbish bin. Then again a Gull had joined the queue at the bus stop, head jerking up and down as it read the timetable with serious concentration. One old lady backed away in alarm.

The Mugsborough animal was a horse, and a Gull was seen riding off down the promenade with the nag complaining loudly about the weight of overfed gulls nowadays. But what drew most attention was when the two Gulls swooped around each other with matching wing beats and squawks, doing a jig of their own, and then waltzing off along the seafront with a wing round each other's waists, the outer wing waving and blowing kisses to the bystanders.

'Well crunch my crabs!' exclaimed Johnny. 'Anyone'd think they were an item.'

'Perhaps they are,' grinned Claire.

Naomi and Tamsin were teasing the Gulls and shrieking when they were pursued or captured. Tamsin hadn't asked any questions when she saw Naomi arrive at school with Mr Corfield. Naomi breezily explained that he was staying with them for a while; and that was all that was said. Now they were running along the prom, jumping up on benches, pestering Ray for candyfloss, and chatting with Angie and Steve. Naomi felt safe in public, but was shy with Brandon at home. She took it out on Lolly sometimes, and clung to her at others. She didn't let her mind dwell on what might be happening. She saw her dad and Zoe arm in arm, and told herself it was okay, Zoe had often been around, she knew her, it was okay, wasn't it...

Several of the side were quietly watching the new couples, commenting politely on how well they were dancing, but with the occasional raised eyebrow.

Ray and Zoe were certainly putting on a performance, with a touch of bravado. Each felt altered, and saw new things in the other. Ray's mind kept running on how he had been in the past, very conscious that this was his third major relationship. This time, he said to himself, this time I must get it right. I've always enjoyed flirting, taking it too far, a tang of danger in the fun. Hard to hold back. But Zoe deserves better. He found a new generosity in himself, and the way he looked at other people. He squeezed Zoe's hand. This is the real thing, he said to himself. This is love.

They were watching Mugsborough dance. He turned to Zoe.

'Impressive, aren't they? Almost makes me want to make a fresh start.'

'Join Mugsborough, you mean?' Zoe's face had a glow of surprise. 'Now that *would* be a challenge. Hm. It'd certainly be something new for us.'

Most of the Mugsborough dancers arrived at the bedecked scout hall around seven, having enjoyed tea or something a little stronger with their Larksea hosts. Charlie Pritchard was feeling expansive, and adopted the role of master of ceremonies as if he was still squire. He broached the hospitality barrel with a flourish, and called 'Let the wild rumpus start!' In fact it took Pete Kershaw and Lolly to provide some tunes as background music before things relaxed.

People were eyeing the buffet and wondering when they could help themselves. Then, weaving into the chatter, they heard a new sound. Accordion music. As it got louder, the conversation died away. Such a French sound! The guests must have arrived.

The door was flung open.

'Les Danseurs Dieppois!' announced a Mugsborough herald. All eyes turned to the door as four odd creatures pranced in, dressed in grubby whites with large red spots dotted over them, and masks with floppy dog ears... rather like...

Brandon was the first to burst out laughing, recognising one of the Mugsborough men in the costume. He started applauding as the four Roy the

Rovers threw bean bags at each other, dancing in a reel, then a hey...

'It's him! It's our Roy!' shouted Biff, and dived into the set, trying to retrieve the little spotted dog which had appeared amongst the bean bags. Roy was hurtled through the air as the Mugsborough dancers tossed him round the room, throwing him to each other, with Larksea making frantic grabs and dives, till there was a virtual scrum down.

Muffled cries of 'I've got him!' and Luke was allowed to get up, thoroughly dishevelled. He held the battered Rover high above his head, and Larksea started cheering. He walked over to Hannah and ceremoniously presented her with the recaptured mascot.

'We must have a toast!' she called.
'To the Rover's return!'
'To Mugsborough!'
'To the Dieppois!'
'To Aunty Mary's canary!'
...and it degenerated from there.

*

May the First, four-thirty a.m. A salty sea fret was swirling round the cliff by the castle, damp and cool, and there was a muffled jingle of bells in the dark. Then Pete Kershaw began to sing:

Hal-an-tow, jolly rumbelow,
We were out, long before the day-o
To welcome in the summer time, to welcome in the day-o
For summer is a-coming in
And winter's gone away-o.

'I hope it bloody well does, I'm freezing,' said Biff as he dumped his coat on the pile on the wet grass. Alex led the shivering dancers out for the ritual of Shepherd's Hey Fieldtown. There were solemn greetings as they set up, and stood quietly for a moment. Then Pete played alone on the whistle, the haunting old melody hanging in the air, unresolved, almost a minor key, as the tune unfolded in the early dawn light. Alex signalled, and they all stepped in, silently, for the slow salute...

...and out. There was some sporadic applause from the bystanders, some of them dressed rather oddly for reasons of their own, and the first magic dispersed. The dancers patted each other on the back, saying, that went well, that'll bring the sun up, got the pauses right this year... and it's twelve up for Shepherd's Hey Bampton, why not...

Zoe walked quietly to the cliff edge alone, the sea whispering below, streaks of paler light in the sky above. She took the leaf from last year's Jack in the Green out of her pocket, and held it momentarily, thinking: peace, Old One, thanks. Thanks for this renewal, all the May stirrings. Soon you'll bring in the spirit of summer...

She cast the fragile leaf gently over the cliff edge, and watched it twirl down, smaller and smaller, till it was out of sight.

Johnny and Claire Rendell were watching the double set, taking sips of rum from their hip flask. Alex and Hannah were leading the two sets facing each other, with the musicians in the middle, Pete, Lolly and little Steve standing close together. Neither was smiling, but their faces had an elated, meditative calm. This was how things ought to be, they felt.

Brandon bounded through the opening greeting with an extra flourish, like his old self. Claire saw him give Lolly a quick wink as he came to the front of the set, facing her as she played her melodion. She beamed at him, and at Alex and Hannah, thinking: these morris folk, they're my extended family, always there when you need them...

Ray and Zoe had paired up at the back and were standing very straight, shoulders back, determined to synchronise their movements. Both sets had a heightened awareness of dancing together, as the dawn light dispelled the mist and caught the white wavers.

'Alex makes a good PM to our Queen Hannah, doesn't he?' said Johnny.

'Just as well two of them can hold it together,' Claire replied wryly. 'What's that line about ragamuffin husbands and rantipoling wives? Ah well.'

'Twizzlers all,' sighed Johnny. 'Still, look on the bright side. It's Jack's time. Can't help feeling hopeful. "Now comes in summer by your power" and all that. Magic.'

He took her arm and handed her the flask. Claire raised it to the dancers.

'To Larksea,' she said.

'To the morris!' said Johnny, taking a warm sip.

They got ready to dance.

It was getting lighter and lighter. The dawn over the east hill was brightening from red to orange to gold.

The sun will be up any minute, thought Alex, glancing at his watch. It's time for Bonny Green. He called for everyone to join in, bystanders too if they liked. Even Naomi stepped up to dance.

There was no reverence in this traditional massed farewell. Alex bellowed, too high a singing note, 'Weeell...' until everyone was yelling with him, then 'Here's to the lasses...' and the raucous singing broke up as the uneven lines of dancers surged across the grass, grinning and making playful gestures, Hannah in the lead. The formation broke into a big, ragged circle, clumsy movements driven forward by exhilaration, and they led off round the edge of the cliff, the first sparkle of sun rising over the far hill.

Hannah wheeled inwards towards the musicians, and the whole company followed, spiralling into the whorl of a giant snail, tighter and tighter, till Alex shouted 'All in!' A great roar went up, all the wavers held high to salute the sun.

Summer summoned.

Acknowledgements

My warmest thanks are due to Roger Dunkley for bringing the clear eye of a widely-published author to the drafts of this book. His advice, thoughts and patience in reading the ongoing versions were a great help in getting the story out of my head and into an approachable form on the page.

Karen and Colin Cater at Hedingham Fair have been generous in their time and support, and sharing their professional expertise.

Gary Smailes at Bubblecow read the first draft and made some useful suggestions.

Finally, thanks to all my friends in the morris, that great family of folk, singing, dancing and celebrating all the seasons of our lives.